THE VIBRATING POND

THE
VIBRATING
POND

NIGEL HOWSE

Library of Congress Control Number: 2021925355

ISBN: 978-1-956094-69-5   (PB)
ISBN: 978-1-956094-70-1   (HB)
ISBN: 978-1-956094-68-8   (E-book)

Some characters and events in this book are fictitious and products of the author's imagination. Any similarity to real persons, living or dead, is coincidental and not intended by the author.

The Universal Breakthrough
15 West 38th Street
New York, NY, 10018, USA

press@theuniversalbreakthrough.com
www.theuniversalbreakthrough.com

Printed in the United States of America

FOREWARD

This is the second edition of THE VIBRATING POND, a collection of fiction short stories written over several years, between 1975 and 2017. This reprint edition is larger, with new materials. The phrase 'Vibrating Pond' derives from my book of poetry titled 'The Hammer Bird,' published in 1985.

Slow Silences
Rings Singing;
Soft Pond,
Vibrating vision.
Fly ecstasy,
Shimmering sky;
Green wings,
Eternal blue.

Further to the previous contents, namely: The River Deben, My First Day At School, A Winter's Tale, A Dog's Life, The Isle Of Halvos, Wolf Pack, Bolip^e, Black Caymen Egwah, VW Vet and Helter Skelter, I have added more of my fiction stories for you to read.

CONTENTS

THE DAWN

A fusion of black, the night postillion reins in the stallions, driving the shining night carriage. Upon halting, the pale palms of his hands are receiving the sun's first dawning light. A maiden rises and runs passing with delicate hesitancy and curtsies, giving to him a single spray of a white lily.

The amiable Sultan bows to daylight, ending his Moon dancing hours lying besides the black mirror of the shimmering lagoon. He tickles a streaming salmon and opens oysters for pearls. Then, running his hand through icy water, parts the white points of the diamond reflecting stars.

Starfishes are metal sapphire torches spreading white phosphorescent light as giant tentacles, reaching upon the fathomless velvet void and creaking branches of trees robed with windows, shadows and cuts disturbing the cloaks of night. A dream-time place and always appealing, trespassing us in untrodden alley ways.

Dawn's Earth goddess springs with maize sheathing limbs; ripening corn are her germinating eyes. Deeply heralds promises and effects from living causeways. So many veils over hidden dimensions of Earth's creation for the living, our flesh reborn.

In dreaming eyes of sleep, dim lit yellow and purple flowers are fastened, life giving enkindling candles triggering flame. At dawn's triumphal light, birds signal chorusing with rising thanksgiving so many songs.

Heavenly planets are drawing forth change, bringing out the potential being of abundance. Expanding flying ghosts everlasting in clocks of celestial bodies sprouting; Earth's sentient light trophic spirits from evolution's seeds.

MITHRAS THE BULL

The Scribe writes script,
As with a cut quill taken from the swan.

The lines are long, lithe, and strong,
Joined with silent black ink
That these vital hard words might tell,
Memorably to a one-day listener,
A true tale to them, done long ago!

Written much further back than the time
Before the Scribes father was born,
And Man descended beside the Bull.

Harkus heard the wolves baying howls,
As the tinder wood faggots kindled afire,

To a built pyre dedicated to Mithras the Bull.

He, the brother to the captors Centaur

Bent by his steaming pots and ancient anvils,
Weighed-up effortlessly his scales beneath vales,
Stretching away to the great Nordic west!

There, giant brown bears tear and uproot oaks
And Thor an angry God, down bolts lightning,
Crackling and bolting surfaces of Fiords.

Mithra's haunches quiver, writhing ritually;

Aglow with pitch, in the darkest most silent night.
The Iron Moon rocks, bathed in the glowing sky.

Bent by steaming pots and ancient anvils,
And madly dancing, Mithras runs,
Shielded with ice at Winter's wild solstice
Above the wolf's tundra.

The stars, worn with drilling rung bells,

Squeal, rushing themselves by Mountain Rowan trees,
And volcanic fires burning rarefying metals.

While in Taurus receives Springs nuptial horn;
The penitent white blossom fills the black thorn.

Bellowing alive, the tirading bull writhes reborn,
As the stars ignite on his fiery red beard!

All of Winters' night is tossed and stormed;

Mithras, like Bacchus exults in all grand chaos,
As the withered Earth, entangles about his horns
Turns to Junes winging Eros,
And Summer's Maiden comes.

FLINTS & GOLD

A man alights from an oared boat,

River fording between marsh and woodland
As evening's darkness
Overtakes the Deben's eastbank skyline.

The land is misting over,

As stealthy night shapes return,
Gathering again over the world.

He stoops and moves,
Grasping and carrying an object in both hands.

B-boying flints dance together,
Flake-off twisting.

Struck forcefully to bear light.
In the clearing Silver birch coppices
Starkly emblazon white over dun coloured sandlings.

The husbandman strikes fiercely.
Clashing cold stone blades cutlass together.

From his energising hands,
Pitting against smiting stone,
Glinting golden showers gleam cascading –
Spinning through daylight's dieing.
High above him,
Appointing is a bright twinkling steady glimmering.
The pole star lights the azure deepening sky.
Alfreid hears his master's voice calling:
"Hear this, all you who are longing, wandering!"
Alfried says: "The King, done with coursing
And rabid hunter's hounds
Dismisses Pagan or Wodin's wars.

Jackal Viking's bent to rid the rood,
Disregard deified man crucified."

A great fire erupts,
Blandishing the distant North Sea.
A voice gravely speaks:
"See the firmament,
Place and person,
Your 'Glory Spear' the King!"

Alfried's watering eyes sear.
Charging forward to battle,

He turns, swerving to mysterious horizons,
Underworlds.

Blazing memories fought for,
Tirelessly made, rise up.

Smelted and smithed gifts return to his side.
Made offerings he served for,
Of kith and Kinship.

Alfried's voice yields from the fires heart:
"A Great living Fire carries afar!"

Driving and clinching the King's majesty - magnet:
Pagan sacrifice and welcoming;
Christian belief grew 'life knowing'.

Buried into the universal,
The ground of rising kingship is born,

Binding the towering round burrens
Each beckon as beacons.

For pilgrims setting and trimming their sails
Towards loves own mysterious journey.

Battle bid away the galvanising hordes,
Drawing the King's body borne-aloft,
From land to anchoring history.

Across abroad wastes and water,
This worthy one so proved;
Restoring to land, upon sandlings.

Of outlying coastal clans,
By yonder whale-water roads each yield,
Paying tribute for a most blessed king.

His vicus regius, Majesty lodged therein.
The Royal timbered Hall at Rendlesham,
Radiant with gold during His reign.

A shining light redolent over many lands
Fostering barter and kingships,
Drew laden treasures of gold.

Jewelry and ceremony, Wargear shields,
Swords with golden helmets.

His faithful followers all cry:
"The Ship is lit and on fire!

We Anglophiles set precedent, Drawing open harbours,
Gathering booming mercantile trade!

Our worldly sights we set-to build,
Across native coasts and wide heralding seas!"
"We set out towards the new horizon."
For the King must bow down before his God,
Grow in stature and defy earth.

In his pyre,
Nearing a higher station,
Received on this island's defending sea,
Open to the horizon evermore.

Sheer in weight,
The ship 90 feet from tip to tail,
Broad swordsmen carrying the hull and nave,
Into earth's safe berth.

Across twelve centuries
His Anglo-Saxon war helmet and shoulder clasps,
Wearing gold and inlaid with precious stones
Placed near the King's head, emerges.

With gold coin offerings,
Passagings for the after life,
A Saxon lyre still plucks woven thralling songs.

THE GYPSY AND THE WELL

The well was at the bottom of the garden and was surrounded by a red brick wall, covered in moss and sweetbriar and honeysuckle. On a bright day, peering into the shadowy depths, the floor could be seen, many feet below. A stream, silver-like trickled along the bottom.

An old, settled gypsy owned the adjoining cottage. His caravan was overgrown now with ivy and grasses clustered around the wheels. His two brown lurcher dogs were housed inside over the night.

The gypsy was a silversmith and read palms for traveller's wayfaring along these parts. Often Bejo, for such was his name, lit a fire in the evening and sat beside the warmth into the morning making tea, and cooking flavoursome meals in his stewing pot. He would smoke at his long pipe and stare watery eyed and unblinking into the fire.

His face was brown and wizened with many lines. All of his people had been Giorgio's. Both his parents and even further back had studied and had a natural talent for magic and foretelling. However, most satisfaction was obtained from his own affinity he had with the fairy folk.

During the daytime, in the very early morning, he opened up the window at the front of the house, after stoking up the forge. He made trinkets, studded with bright coloured glass gemstones and sold them to whoever looked in.

Long ago, when young, Bejo had helped his father smith and dig for the small silver nougats. On full moon or quarter moon nights, the hunt for silver began. Deidre was learned and old, a queen who dressed herself all over with refined and ancient gypsy silverware.

She led the hunt. She had long silvery grey hair, very dark eyes, long fingernails and a piercing look on her face. She walked barefoot and wore a long black cotton dress, studded, and threaded with silver and rare stones.

She said that the fairy folk on the night of the full or quarterly moon, travelled far and wide in the countryside by its light. They wove spells and flew upon its energy. Strangest of all, they also keep this energy, breaking off pieces and substance under the turfs.

Deidre, whose sole time was spent pursuing the lost light of the moon, spent long hours in the night studying the ground, sometimes going off alone on long walks away from the camp.

She indicated her triumph by the blowing of her sound-less whistles; whereupon all the camp dogs were unleashed on the hunt. The foraging party followed on behind.

This much, Bejo could remember. He had been very close to Deidre. On her deathbed, before she had died, she had told him of a promise. This promise was a tremendous secret to those gypsies. He had learned from her about this cottage. And of the well.

By starlight, he had spent his youth walking through a giant forest, until he heard the exact whereabouts of the well and eventually found its locality. And had parked his van by its lonesome domain, relieved to be settled where the smithing could be done.

The fairies were there all right; in a giant ring they performed their liquid-silver ceremonies, having traditionally always done so by this well. They kept the stream alive in the well. Bejo lay special offerings of his silver jewellery pieces by it once a month.

He spent many long hours creating minute necklaces and tiaras, stars, maces, and orbs, burnishing and polishing them until they shone brightly as the constellations. Then he placed each piece in a ring, circling around the well. Always with stealth and in secrecy, the fairies would come and take one piece they had chosen.

And in return, silver of such sweet richness was available afterwards. Bejo knew that the fairies were highly pleased. And so it was, the gypsies craft of smithing continued, making brooches and candlesticks, spoons and caskets, all bright and of moon silver.

Furthermore, it is more than rumour, that this gives good fortune, for it is the stuff of the fairy folks; of those who tipped the bright moon into the well!

THE ISLE OF HALVOS

The sky was busy all day long, flocked with honey bees. Their land here was a green place; always the sun shone amongst the gardens, between the mountains of Halvos.

The Lords of the Canton lived in their palaces, built of sugar and their crystallised walls shone brightly in the daylight. The dwarf slaves, peculiar to this island, were employed in the court and had especially clever small hands and limbs. They landscaped the gardens, encouraging many plants and herbs to scent and blossom abundantly.

Often though, sloths with especially long tongues gallivanted through the walkways in the early hours or after dusk, when the crowing clock had rested-up his beak. Along these crystal demerara beds of sugar, these lemurs then slid, chomping up the candied lily heads. How they relished these parks, all the honey, the summer houses, rockeries sundials and the bell-towers.

The Lords were forever busy, making bricks out of beeswax, modelling new garden seats to replace those eaten up by the sloths or lizards and moths. On several gift days, the parlour-maids made syrup balls, mixed with cherry nougat, and these were hung up on the pomegranate trees. They were for the sloths and so kept them from eating up the palaces and other things.

One day in Summer, the Tulp arrived in their midst, whilst the Lords were seated together, sipping meads. All were drowsily bemused by the droning of the bees. The Tulp was tall and they were short. He rode a thin shanked pony and they never before had seen its kind. Tulp wore a Turkish Fez and purple breeches and an eye-glass was set precariously in his left eye, fixing him with an inquisitive gaze.

Under his right arm he had brought a large book, whose pages held many wonders and secrets. Books were unknown to them, for the Lords were simple men. The Tulp entertained with his book; each page held innumerable pictures. These he would take and show on his lantern, lit by sunflower oil and projected against the covering of the royal Caliph's own bed. The Caliph, being the oldest Lord, slept there always, awaking only as a rare blue moon emerged above his bed. Turning after, a blush pink!

The images brightly flickered upon the cloth-covering, as clowns in kaleidoscopic dress, with fauns and dancers captivating to entrance them. Other strange lands, unknown customs and pageantries dazzled and perplexed the noble audience. By Tulp's magic lantern, night after night, the Lords and their princely son's eagerly took to their cushions, as Tulp delved deeper into his book.

In the passing of these timely pastimes the royal gardens grew wild. Fountains in the park trickled haphazardly. Sloths moving about unchallenged, ate the sweet waxy receptacles over-strewn with scented trailing flowers. The Lords grew deaf to the lizards and sloths munching and scrunching, licking closer and nearer to their doors. Long before Tulp had turned his last page, the lizards nibbled upwards, nimbly reaching the palace tiles.

So engrossed in the lantern show, the Lords were blind also to the bees' plight, having so little blossom, producing little honey. And so there was of course a drastic shortage of wax and bricks.

One day, whilst the day was young and the Lords were out fashioning new seats in the honeysuckle gardens, Tulp packed up his lantern and slipped away. The palace was in uproar. The hallways were in ruins; ants cavorted on the piled scree of the walls. Monkeys chipped off mouthfuls of the rafters before leaping back into the garden's wilderness. And a honey bear had already eaten the pantry in the kitchen, before reaching for the oven made of delicious tasting hard syrup.

Then a trumpet called and the Lords of the Canton, standing outside in their gardens became afraid. The Vabods had come and the Stone men would follow, riding their yellow war horses. Their pet leopards were the most feared. Leased and purring, but scaring the humming birds out of their nests.

Already, the Vabods feathered war bonnets, apparelled with hawk, eagle and goose quills were sighted from the look-out pavilions above the snow. With haste, the Lords bade farewell to their slaves and their caparison of maids in waiting, including the birds within the music room and the queen bee hives. Garbing their bare feet in walking moccasins, the royal entourage fled away, as the stone men entered at the south gate.

The ravenously hungry leopards immediately scented the chocolate and spices from the palace kitchen and roared out, joined by the war banshee of the warriors. As the palace was now in ruin and the roof much crumbled into decay, the sound of their voices was more tumultuous than a storm at sea. Badly shook the roof. The grey stone men ambled into the Great room and they opened and banged all the thin doors.

The Vabods were also hungry after their arduous journey rowing the seas without any food or sleep. They snatched at the tastily decked chandelier hanging above them and each pulled greedily for a share, for each warrior was impatient with hunger. They tussled and heaved, each jostling to fight for a larger share, contesting against the might of the other, as against a foe. They lunged and they swung and pulled heaving again. Then it happened; the roof creaked and groaned and fell!

The monkeys screeched, while the parakeets leapt into the air with a flurry of bright features. And the sloths, not now so slow, rolled off the eaves of the roof. Beneath the roofs smitten tiles and the choking dust, it was another story! No Vabod, no Stonemen, nor strong angry leopards escaped from these spreading tiles covering and crushing them. Instantly this fall marked the end of the Vabod army, determined to pillage the Canton of Halvos.

Eventually, the Lords of the Canton, now far away, heard word of these events, taking their long red boats back into the mist, always hanging between the mainland and the passage to their island. The lords of the Canton would return again, making peaceful and busy residence with the kingdom of the bees. Already the sloths were licking their lips in greedy anticipation of their homecoming.

BEACH STORY

I am a set loose small Limpet crab, beetle browed and white shelled. I have heard it whispered by a yawning oyster shell that it is the seventh of July today and too frenzied and hot grows the sun. The suns' dazzling radiations emblazon all corners of the ground beyond the hem of the sea.

I was born here at Felixstowe and beneath these groynes is my home. During this season I am surrounded by a stampede and wall of trespassers worshipping the sun.

I know it is afternoon, past meridian, because I perceive the out-going tide, the slant nearer to the earth of the sun and the growing feeling of the more cool, calm waves.

Now at two o'clock, it is past picnic time for the languishing and lazy humanoids. I have crept away from the heat and the peering eyes of so many holidaying, the children and their yapping, tail wagging scatty dogs.

Beneath the pier I lie, looking out from my shadowed recess, even now too warmly air-wafted and lapped with small, heated wavelets.

I had spent the morning sucking at some cod paste sandwiches and other dainty morsels, strewn from an extraordinary surfeit of food hampers.

Between the all too busy times of relishing this abundant bouquet of flavours, ie sauces of sour cheese, stinking sauerkraut, combined with the jetsam of semolina and lettuce leaves, scuppered beneath a dainty trellis of fried chicken, my straining eyes viewed the droves of new arrivals with disturbed amusement.

My main satisfaction was in watching them, these passing strangers with their restless, not always predictable antics and their shapes and ways and the incessant murmur of voices. They arrive like a stream, the numbers continuously make a wave.

As the day wears on, the sea catches them unawares and charms them all, soothing their consciousness with an overwhelming and suffusing drowsiness.

One moment they are standing, and while I only for one moment am listening to the bubbles tunefully running through a sea-grass shell, they are suddenly lying along the sand, staring out to the horizon.

At the moment though, next to these multitudes of ant-like creatures, I seem like a giant whale, lolling in the water. That is why I crow, laughing as they queue for drinking water at the Spa's iron tap.

I know too that the silver-coloured sand is baking hot. These pink, almost naked animals are as many today as the pebbles on the beach. Indeed, as plentiful they are as my distant cousins, the sea lions, with their flippers lying shoulder next to shoulder.

The old ones sit poised on canvas, slung over shaped wooden seats. I sometimes can hear them snoozing from beneath their black-lined large napkins.

At sun-down the pickings begin, when I shall wrestle with the star-fishes, crumpled cornets and exotic bananas, stuck to crisps. Then this populace will have retired, and the beach will be empty again as a desert and my relief shall be embraced by the slow sounds of the becalming sea.

It is confusing when I sometimes stop to think about what is happening today. I smell and see such strange things.

For instance, the sky is full of whirling shapes in many colours and in front of me a little child, evidently pleased, points at them with his fingers and squeals "kites"!

I hear too, the wooden hinged motion of the oars in the row-locks of small fishing boats. Where do these smells arise? Fruit intermingles with sweet rock and black bubbling tar.

Red-faced persons lick a sickly dripping white substance and rub brown smearing stuff over their limbs. Their feet seem to pray up towards the heavens.

They seem to quickly tire and lie down motionless, after swimming in the water, wrapping themselves in rainbows of cloth. I cannot fathom any reason for much of what they do!

Perhaps I must not try so hard to explain; there is the sleeping, sighing music of the sea, so calming in the heat l am still so hot and it feels deep down so cool. The people are hot too.

Some of their naked feet cannot stand it; their faces become howling and grimacing as they try to tip-toe over the burning shingle. Along the town front, the shops are sun-shaded by canopies. The doors are open wide as if to help regain their breathing.

Perhaps the shopkeepers, who incidentally never come out, are on their knees, sucking ice lollies and cooling themselves with the many buzzing air-fans!

MY FIRST DAY AT SCHOOL

Old Melton C.P. School is a Victorian building, made redundant for a long time now. It is built in two parts. One is for us infants, where I started on this day. For two formative years we stayed here under Miss Ward's tutelage. Then we crossed over to the main building to continue our studies. This similarly was split into two parts. From ages seven to nine, and then nine through to eleven, six years altogether. This final primary phase was under Mr Bruce, the Headmaster.

Alongside Wood's Lane, our road cement pillar's like grey teeth ranged the roadside. Each was pierced with rusty wire, twisty like crusty-brown rolled tobacco. The quarter mile to school skipped and twisted back and forth. On the left appeared the Council estate, grey and all uniformly plain, none individually painted as it is today! And like a continuing scene from our garden at home, the road path was bordered with ornamental Rowan trees. The road man kept the grass verges trim, scything by hand mostly.

On the main road's other side, Bloss the farmer kept his pasture for horses. Like other children from the estate, afternoon's after school we see-sawed on low horse-chestnut tree boughs. On mornings going to school, we played somersaults rolling ourselves over the wires. We fished in 'bomb-hole' ponds in the fields. In late Spring to Autumn, the spot being low and damp, filled with buttercups.

The tarmac footpath blistered in places like nut-brittle, or fat shiny licorice. Off-white fungi amazingly cracked on through. My sister Kita bent to tie her shoelaces. Then she stood up, pausing to arrange her satchel behind. Instantly she tightly held the fence's wires, launching herself over them. She laughed as she landed, cart-wheeling upside down back on the roadside.

My oldest sister Yvonne, at ten, with one more year left in primary led the way. Unlike her and Markita, I hadn't the experience of starting primary school. This was the Autumn term in '57. We had arrived at Melton village from Orford earlier that summer holiday. Over-cocooned in my security, I felt myself waking now to all this new life milling around.

The narrow country road filtered fast with heavy traffic. Alongside, milling out from houses, we dawdled and crawled, moving forwards inexorably, towards an unknown place. Most American 'Base' vehicles passed, coming thick and fast. Buicks, Cadillacs and Pontiacs swished past, interspersed with seaweed-green camouflaged military fuel tank-carriers. From Bentwaters, hugely bright coloured metallic chromed cars steamed by.

A figure came into view. She wore a white cap over her black curly hair. Holding up a long mace, as though standing attention like a guard, her white shiny coat stretched to the ground. Later, I learnt this friendly helper was the lollipop lady! She smiled and endlessly crossed and recrossed the road, assisting parents and children.

Opposite to the school gates was the village shop, mecca for gob-stoppers, sweets, aniseed balls, sherbet dips and the myriad penny box treats!

To me, the school built of red bricks gave hints of a prison compound. Taller than adults, castle walls surrounded us. No sooner inside the premises, I felt menaced by its enclosure. Powerless, I looked up, knowing I could neither look over or hope to climb them. Yet I soon did both, like all the rest!

The large tarmac playground went right around the sprawling building, sloping gradually away. I had never before seen such a big black yard. My sisters disappeared, merging with their established friends. Now I felt dwarfed and alone, amongst so many crowding bodies and unfamiliar faces.

Later I enjoyed the free-for-all tumble on these slopes and wintry slides. My head was all a fizzle amongst this cavalcade of games. Of hop-scotching and clowning, skipping, game-swapping and marbles. So we played ricocheting foot and hand-balls, spinning into the air …

Loudly the children's voices echoed excitedly, like whirling birds calling as they flew past, recoiling off the walls. Looping hoops, reverberating with them amidst our squealing.

The playground's spell was broken by a gloved pupil emerging from around the corner of the main building. In her hand she was holding a tinkling object. She broke into an awkward run, then earnestly shook the clanging break-ending bell. CLANG a' CLANG!!! This loud clamour marked the play-time ending. Now at 9am began another passage, drawing us inside to sit down and start the daytime classes.

I entered the building through a gothic green painted hinged door. We hung our coats on metal coat pegs. I saw and smelt the cloakroom's red polished parquet flooring. The white-enamel hand basins were all shiny. My senses drank in the blisters of red carbolic soap. The roll of thin dry, yet soiled towelling lifted and clanged, as I tried to draw it down. Miss Ward steered us charges through her washroom …All our freshened-clammy hands now pinched clean.

We were ushered to sit down on light wooden form benches. We had arrived in our classroom! I smelt and felt the warm glow of the room. My eyes took in the large bright space, of the wooden panelling below tall casement windows.

Miss Ward placed children's paintings on the whitewashed walls. Also, next to her blackboard, centrally stood the blackened solid-fuel stove. Like a man's sooty pipe, its funnel was bedded into the wall. Surrounded by a tall silver-coloured, meshed fire-guard, the fire was always lit and heated the whole classroom. Filled coke skittles stood ready.

I sensed my own small presence here, underscored by realising I was quite unknown to all these strangers here. Yet I had my wits about me, I looked about the place. I found I had the courage to listen to my own voice. I noticed filled coloured boxes on the floor; my happiness lifted, I saw toys!

Our new faces no sooner arrayed there, when a loud wretched wailing arose. Miss Ward interceded, was both soothing and adding foreboding. "Cherry Wilson, come now. There, there. Cease your crying! "Her voice was warm and firm. I was surprised she knew her name! I guessed uneasily she had mine!

'Miss' moved in close to her with mollifying tenderness. Yet Cherry wasn't ready to be outdone. Quivers of choking, cries uneasily creased her pink round face. The flooding tears splashed like rain. Miss Ward calmly assuaged her, as we all sat squirming on the wooden form. Were all like freshly arrived migrant birds, emergent from our more familiar territories and thresholds.

Miss Ward had bright eyes, within a rather puckered worn face. Blue and firm, they were mixed with stern friendliness. She always wore a grey and neat suited skirt with brown office-type brogue shoes. Her top was mostly a white ironed blouse. Sometimes this was a soft pastel colour, of light pink or blue. And also she had on a grey or pringle light blue cardigan. I remember seeing a gold and enamel brooch on her left lapel.

Quite short, even to us children, she seemed a bit of a tyrant. Her rather severe grey short hair, parted on the right side with a hair grip, was cut neatly beneath her ears. Powder masked grey on her pink turning skin, lined and furrowed by years of care. Her voice, while dry, emoted care. As all children commonly share their knowledge, we all criticised never openly, the dank unsavouriness of Miss Wards 'mustard' smelling breath!

Here in class was the watching and sit-up and begging times. Soon after nine, the morning milkman clattered and banged thuds of metal crates. Left outside the rear hallway for us always famished kids, these were filled up with half-pints on the coconut mat. Greedily I also eyed the few samples of gold-capped 'panda' orange juice.

Miss Singleton, the cash lady, arrived for collecting the class dinner money. Her fir-green coloured nylon work tunic seemed uniform and strange. Wearing bright red lipstick, she always smiled, looking straight into our faces. She had blond curls, a big bright round face, wearing round gold earrings. You could hear her white stiletto heels come clicking down the stone flooring. Miss Singleton's silhouette appeared first behind the yellow frieze of the door's window before she entered the room.

"Please Miss, can I be excused? I want the toilet!" Like flotillas of rabbits, each child by turns bounded out! There were, I soon discovered, two toilet systems. Both at the front, beside the bicycle shed and the coke pile, next to the seniors. At the rear, in the playground's corner, was the boys' open urinal. Smelling sourly from torrented stale piss, it made its shiny wall so slimy. It was my ambition to shoot the highest! The floor was cement and always smeary wet.

Sometimes it improved when the cleaner poured jays-liquid down, sanitising with a pitch smell I found strangely-always so satisfying. The black liquefied to grey, curdling. What was so often a compelling swift visit became for a short time far less repellent though still unsavoury.

Nearly next to this portal were brick toilet huts looking like big lambs hutches. Inside, set side by side, open all together with about seven or eight wooden loos. These worn, warm pine seats had blackened; unflushing bent fouled buckets stowed beneath them, gathering up stinking stashed spoors …

We had exercises outside on black rubber mats, kept in a cupboard with green doors. Each took turns lifting one out. The black mat squirmed, folding coldly against my naked legs like a snake. When we sat, the ground beneath was so uncomfortable, the hardness bit and tormented so much one could barely sit still. All the instructed class moved and choreographed, like jerking clocks ticking together. We watched breathlessly, listening and keeping time to Miss Ward's instructions.

In the seniors' house, lunches were served in the refectory, brought in by people with hot food trolleys. Then the rest of the school in the playground and classrooms became still, void of usual hubbub. At lunchtime our family went home. Before going, I drew in the steamy wafts of sickly boiled cabbage, the clatter of stainless steel pans and servers. The nearest I got to ever having dinners at school was when I brought a packed lunch.

Boiled rice pudding gulped and grace no sooner said, we returned in the blink of an eye! All the dinner tables were tidied away, to go frolicking outside. We played beneath the sheltering tall old willow tree, overhanging the right side wall. Long shadows stretched, lengthening there in mid-afternoon.

The rest of the afternoon had another pace to it. Less urgently, the radio Home programme was turned to 'listen with mother', and we sat on the floor entranced with voices and imaginings, toys and puzzles.

When we assembled for afternoon music class, Miss Ward brought out a box of musical instruments. I chose a big tambourine to rattle, then beat an oily stretched skin drum. I saw she sat at the new piano and also sang. And we, so keen to keep rhythm, bleated, rattled and wailed.

The swift brass pendulum shining soft as syrup inside the classroom's octagonal clock, slipped to three-thirty. Time mysteriously had surged forwards. Slipping so, a new avenue beckoned. My blue mack was tugged on, again I found my form. My red-scuffed ready knees below my flannel shorts shot forwards. Who needed the voice? "Children, don't run!" That day, we all waited for each other and left school together.

Homeward we trod. I had heard while out in the playground the squealing pigs from Friar's butchery. Someone said "Them's pigs are for sausages being slaughtered now!" It was done behind Friar's sweet shop. Next we passed the murky brown Gaol building that once held Dutch prisoners for hanging, captured from Southwold's battle of Sole Bay.

Mr Van Someren, another Dutchman, was alive then. Fronting Melton House, I spied the old artist wearing his straw hat, His head was bent patiently over the easel through his shady window.

We strolled on, passing the old Magistrates coffee house, and the magnificent tall grey-trunked beeches. Beeches' was the house where Thomas Churchyard, a local nineteenth century artist, had lived. With my lighter satchel rocking on my shoulders and a stick in my hand I scratched the brick wall.

I raced on in my sister's footsteps; hurrying to watch the 'Lone-Ranger and Tonto' on television at Mr Baker's bungalow before our tea...

EARTHEN WARES

Gigantium Signor Apertifi the miller, tore apart with urgent hungriness another floury fresh baked loaf; slipping pieces fitfully, of white parmesan cheese into his already stuffed ample mouth.

His son Periot, ever gregarious, large, and cheerful, carried. the emptied wine caskets into the basement scullery, where the liquors lay stored. Since he had worked in the mill, Periot had customarily drank the wine of the picked grapes, taken from their own local grove over the years.

How much he relished the sup and swilling sensation gushing out of control as his throat gargled. It almost hurt and tasted like mustard when he over hurriedly swallowed it. His tongue at most times looked like an over-ripe boiled bill bury, swollen with these bitter sour to sweet juices.

But he didn't escape to this quenching bacchic parlour every hour of day. Often the sun grew furiously hot, and he and his father rallied furiously, keeping their bodies busy with the turning, grinding wheel, from sun awakening to the tiresome dusk, by winds rushing in from the sea, thrusting around the wooden sails.

Autumn harvesting had begun. Apertifi with Periot in his granaries, thrashed and flailed the stack-cut corns, sending crisp husks and dried broken leaves scattering onto the powdery-stone white floor. Apertifi panted and blew, dragging breathlessly his flail with wearied long arms, patiently beating down in frequent rhythms.

Suddenly, with muffled puffs, he would stop and wipe his tanned wet brow, drawing himself up. Then with a swift, thoughtful turn, he paused to shift his weight and remove the dross from off his feet, only to continue cudgelling the sheafs.

The grain trickled away, shifting like glistening beetles, sliding into the depressed gully in the wall. In there it met the rolling granite stones, slowly wearing down the kernels and grinding these golden centres, into heaps of cinnamon shaded flours.

Periot and Apertifi worked together ceaselessly to crush laden wheat and maize and winnow, leaving the heaps of waste to dry off for later burning. All the while, the tides of village farmers arrived with great loads on their wooden tumbrels. Apertifi would eagerly hasten with gleeful excitement, remonstrating and gesticulating with his hands to meet each farmer alone, without Periot.

Periot was not there, no! Apertifi shook his head, placating his own indisputable position. Apertifi had profited considerably by his own arrangements They were both alike, but in Bonafede the Sicilian miller would be the top-rooster, in his house of labour.

So, son Periot sacked up and sewed the flours and stacked the sacks, sweating much -as he did so. Only the hefty cracking beams in the dry heat of the mill, broke the silence of the active, white-shrouded men.

As Autumn bore in upon them, they both quietly worked on, the father in the winnowing room above his son.

Every morning first thing, before the sun arose, Periot fed their rococo cockerels' red strutting fellows down in the hop drying sheds. He collected the leather carrying grain bags from the end of Apertifi 's bed and tiptoed out, down the round stone stair-case of the Villa, to the granary silos for some spare grain.

To Periot, these scarlet birds were a special passion to him: their powerful wings and their long throats, reaching forth so high, exclaiming their jagged, impatient notes.

The ground about them was littered with feathers. When they fought, it looked like flames flickering out from a volcano. Their sleek bodies swept the floor as they pranced to and fro and would crow out at Periot so fiercely when they saw him coming up to them with food, he often felt afraid before them.

The eight-rococo cockerels were so evenly matched, that despite their duels, dashing and going into the other, they were rarely hurt.

Apertifi too, wisely understood that such spirited contests were more for prideful show than for murderous vents of their zeal. As far back as he could remember, his family and all of his forefathers, who had also been millers, had always kept rococo cockerels rarely had they died.

What was very strange: every time his relatives had died, another red cockerel appeared from nowhere!

The mill wheels grinded many harvest yields and the years rolled by. And so Periot, learning his trade, gradually took charge of the greater burdens, looking to the upkeep of the mill.

Apertifi was getting old. At market, his eyesight longer matched his friends and failed to distinguish the grain types separately. How that angered him, for it could lose him his renowned trade.

Somehow the handling of grain was to be left in his charge; he became unpopular and greedy. Things got muddled and more difficult for Periot.

Because Apertifi made mistakes and foolishly blamed Periot for them, often in front of the farmers, mistrust and suspicions in the men grew. Their yields, entrusted to Apertifi by them to regrade and refine them, became mixed up and poorly milled.

Gradually discontent amongst them grew and with the deepening disaffection, the mill fell out of favour; consequently it lost many of its benefits of trade. Apertifi more frequently squandered his time, drinking upon his back within the mill, staring out vacantly across the daily changing colours of his empty vineyard. Periots' daily work shortened and his time too became gloomily spent, idly plucking unripened grapes and talking to the cockerels.

How sad was the mill; how troubling it was to him, his fathers health and the slack conditions of the business. So disturbed, he clapped his hands and realised his fortune and strength was ebbing away from him.

It was an ordinary September day, and the harvest would soon begin. The grapes hung heavily ripe, all soon ready for picking. By his feet stood the cockerels, each stationary, each strangely silent and intent. They collectively looked up at his face and then down at their taloned feet.

Beside each of them, lying in the dry sand, in neat rows, glistened twelve long rows of gleaming grains, each one graded in type, size and in quality! Each pile was the selected yield-sample of the local farmer's harvest.

Periot, totally dumbfounded, with necessity found he had to rouse himself to his better senses; he pinched his nose, howling thankfully into the air. For a full hour he leaned against his staff, blinking and bowed with incredulity over his treasure in dismay. The rococo's always were extraordinary; now in this time of their hopelessness, he had at last discovered their mystery!

In great pride, he gathered up the grains, tucking each separate pile of grains in a silk handkerchief. Now he knew that neither the mill would fail and that his father Apertifi, need not die in bitterness and failure.

And so it was; the grain that harvest time flooded through their gates, very plentiful like abundant rain again. And even Apertifi, knowing better fortune from their discovery, became more gracious towards his son.

Both shared the bird's secret, and soon in celebration, the old miller decided on his ground, there would be a festival. There would be heaps of fruit and deliciously cooked meats, washed down by many jugs of vintage wines, together with fiddle music and much dancing in the streets on harvest Moon festival!

And all of the time, Periot at early dawn whispered his gratitude to the mill's guardians, the eight rococo cockeral's. And loud and exclamatory was their prideful crowing in the yard!

THE POND

"Unafraid and girdled in the serpent, she passed through the waters unharmed."

The peak-nosed, poking-pike, prowls and stoops into the green navel and harbour of this upside-down world, of nets and ships; re-floating and often wracked, again setting sail. All are gathered into the caverns, recesses, and the rippling shadows.

The soft Moon sails above, marking time, plotting the course and compasses of dissolution, of the myriads in their spawning blue waters. Here's becalmed Ithaca, and here also lies the green goddess of the pond.

Many spell-bound brown frogs are hidden in the sedges, listening to the showers of the mermaid's music, whispering crystal bubbles into the water's edge. Within its reaches lie festoons of stuff, slime green hair, sea-lettuce, Prospero's skull, and a necklace of tangling weeds.

The fish and three-fingered gods weave their spreading inks and written dreams here. So too, the birth of Carthage and other ancient cities found their being and other Eden's.

The white rumbling wagons alive in calm motion, where insects send forth dragon flies; the stars of planes embellishing the airways and the eyes of fish move their slow tails and pause ponderously. The shy pond world encloses the hooded shell; fins under pinioned ferns; the hook claws.

A man's overhanging habitation towers and is submerged with the stooping children, reflecting. They go dangling their fishing lines into the waters, of themselves...

The Summer Pond is a place of silences and spheres of changing festivity. Yet the Winter Pond, as icy as the cold north, then becomes despotic as a grey Scandinavian witch, casting her cruel frozen spells.

Daily in the pond are inscribed the passing messages of the seasons. Creation is over the rock shoulders, as the seed sparkles; the rainbow shimmering the mirrors.

And the Summer swallows shake over the breaking hands of the clouds, always returning. They go echoing and resounding, while the water bison, fish, fly, beast and fauna, live and lap, leaping from darkness.

The newts wend over the flower-scattered bridge above succulent green-lilies bestowing themselves; the vegetable growth flowering and sowing, all covered with gliding, water lapped snails.

So too with man; the pond gives passage to his laden dreams. And Jonah, passing from the whale, did forgo his fear of drowning.

STALLIONS BITE

Georgio clipped ten minutes over the rest, despite the foul conditions. Only seasoned punters glimpsed through the rain black threading haunches kicking high. The stallion thundered, snorting triumphantly. Thrashing the course. Dunstan's all those four furlongs had plunged into mud. Yet Georgio, when he flew home drew little fiery applause from his drenched owner O' Leary.

"I'll crush your teeth" is all he shouted, The beer tent belched cavorting figures, slithering upon the mud. The horse's race primed the men.

Broth of the porter helped them lunge off their feet.

"Catch that one for a hearty relish" spewed Laurie. His teeth tinged with blood.

O'Leary, as a boy in Driscoll's tannery shop, where the cockatoo loomed large, talking to him. It was green and suspended upside down from the cage. O'Leary also loved listening to the whisper from inside his Grandfather Petherwin's Gladstone bag. The polished artifact he carried was a stallion's skull. The Granddaddy of them all, fiery Benadowr.

Great Dublin winner of the l794 Irish Sweepstake.

It spoke sourest and sweetest deprecations. Mostly in a growling, Irish soft burred accent. "Mother loves you. The master should be horsewhipped. I'll lead you past the post first, along Nought street…

This skull was the progenitor in O'Leary's life. Leading him out down long forgotten roads. Petherwin was well versed in this curious horsemanship.

"Many a time had I galloped across the sylvan moors, borne up by the mighty stallion's power taken out of doors. Whatsoever we run, a strange affliction occurs."

In his diaries, Petherwin wrote "These legs fall, come dependent on men."

Benadowr said "My dear sir, what nonsense! Our roving step is compelled only by music. I attended once at Handel's magisterial Court."

Was it a strange quirk that O'Leary should remember the skull when he grew up? Then meeting his sweetheart, a second Marguerite.

For so long Petherwin had forgotten the skull. It lay gathering dust in the racing club's museum. O'Leary had heard the tale, how his grandfather had high-tailed out the museum, wearing the horse's head. A long tradition of romantic trysts, preluding the settlements of married happy life. Since the time when his own fortunes had changed, finishing his veterinary training and had started courting.

Is it possible yet, that a horse falls head over heels for a girl? Fiery Benadowr told Petherwin such a love had existed. Handel had a cousin named Marguerite, who managed and then rode Derby winners, jockeying this great horse.

After Georgio's win, celebrations at the end of the day's racing. Often a butt of jokes at his 'wobbling horse box', and how Georgio must 'have got the right shoes on his left feet' at last!

O'Leary was on the up. The extra imbibed spirits sparkling, despite the jag on his jaw and all. As they left the course, with the wind and rain falling heavily, dark drew in swiftly.

"We did it" O'Leary called up his sweetheart Marguerite, lifting the phone receiver from its compartment, the skull of Benadowr. Marguerite hadn't been able to come over from America; her parents were ill.

"How marvellous" she laughed. "Well done! Kiss Georgio for me, won't you."

O'Leary was resourceful if nothing else. The trailers' loose wheel finally wobbled off. The van turned half-turtle into the ditch. He'd stumbled out, clutching the tool chest under his right arm. He also took the phone, protected by the skull. Slipping the phone into his pocket as the rain lashed down, O'Leary placed the skull onto his head for protection.

Just as he was pumping up the jack, a motor cyclist skidded past, catching O'Leary's toolbox, knocking him out. Sending him with the bowling motorist, headlong down into the ravine. The horse's skull saved him from crushing his own head. He'd fallen heavily.

As he pitched forwards, the familiar voice of Benadowr stirred; it's hot breath flowing into his ears. "I'll run the distance Marguerite!"

The green cockatoo's feathers had tickled O'Leary's nose. Making him sneeze violently as it bent low answering Benadowr's question. 'How Marguerite had chosen the bright red feathers for her bonnet'

The cockatoo, O'Leary saw, became raucous, answering "Why you're one to talk. You visited America long before I was even an egg inside my mother's womb!"

"My great Grandparents were natives of Virginia!" Benadowr said.

"And we carried you back. Marguerite loved the Virginian races. More so its wildlife. Rather than kill birds for feathers, she fondly brought you as a pet. Here you have stayed since. But I know we desire the same in spirit. To journey back, running freely through those woods."

The cockatoo replied, "You are a fine fellow; we shall return again…"

The Indians wore yellow snake-skin headbands and bartered with Virginian tobacco. Peace treaties they said were not enough. They had come to honour the white King, George 2 They understood Chiefs are powerful. All of Virginia was a bustle of people. The climate of fear changed.

The King and all his Yeoman Guard had arrived. In the pearly grey light of dawn, vast white sailed schooners, like fish eagles had swooped in.

Through camouflage at the edge of the forest, the Indians had gathered. Gazing hard to absorb everything.

Marguerite had returned. She would speak to the King, as the Indians' friend and spokeswomen. She knew who and what had harmed them. But first, on their own horse, the fiery Benadowr must race and win!

Marguerite knew that there was something wrong when she was woken up by a loud cawing sound, whirling about outside her apartment. A green cockatoo was knocking annoyingly against her window, as though trying to get her attention! Then, after noticing it was 5.30 am, it crossed her mind that this bird looked, yes, reminded her of the same cockatoo in Nought Street, Dublin.

Then she wondered, 'O'Leary hasn't phoned. He said he'd ring when he gets home. I hope he and Georgio's safe!'

As she lifted up her phone, she turned her television on, announcing news from England. There had been a road accident… Georgio had disappeared with O'Leary. "And 'why' "she quailed, "wasn't he answering now? I'll fly to England!"

While many found a pact with white settlers to retain America's Independence, hosts of Indians sided against the King to save the colony. On the day of the King's arrival, he had personally blessed and attended Marguerite's wedding to Lord Petherwn, nephew to Handel. He announced, "1 am so thrilled also with your horse, fiery Benadowr, Great Chief Wengio's horse."

Marguerite begged for the King's private audience. She implored "there will my Lord soon be bloodletting. The Indians are fighting for their rights."

The King puffed out his red cheeks, choking his words. "Yes: there are seditious acts in..h'em..lower ranks. I'll weed them out."

After the celebrated Virginian races, Marguerite and Petherwn fled, together with Benadowr. Soon after, the American settlers rose up, driving the King and his dwindling army into the harbour. The horse, withdrawing with them, whinnied softly as Marguerite cried, nursing all their hurt. An Indians arrow had pierced the horse's side, embedded close to Benadowr's heart.

PINK EARS

Tatum remembers the first photo Greg sent, arriving at school in West Vermont primary. Miss Enright on the first term told all the class: "Our assignment is to get some pen-friends."

She stood in front of the class, opening a world map. "America" she said" is one frontier, but here you can reach out, make friends with others your own age in other countries!"

Hands shot up, everyone was excited, wanting to do this. Miss Enright explains "We can translate languages and incoming messages." She speaks about old 'Esperanto', sign-language like semaphore, or morse. "Using universal images, directly helping talk or communication just-as-well."

Greg: "Yes, I got the pick-up, this one you had sent. It was no ordinary shell, pink and shaped like an ear. I joked at first - 'radiation.' Was it a real body part? Yukhh! All I wanted was white oyster shells for the aquarium! I'd already thrown lots of broken oyster shells away as I trudged about searching. I picked this one up as a novelty; I even found another. A pink pair, ear-shaped. One was enough. I threw the second back into the water!"

"Yes" said Tatum. "Miss Enright was so right. She had come up with this 'distance device' she called it. Sending two shells floating away at the same time synchronises the parallel process. "You'll see" she said, "The second one returns to the sender, because it is a law of nature…"

"When I got home" Greg explains, "I set up my aquarium with all the selection of shells and the fish. The pink shell looked different although I knew it to be an oyster shell. Hidden inside, I found a very tiny black oyster. That first night I had propped it beside the fish tank. Something about it grabbed my attention. Holding it to my ear drew natural yet definite sounds."

"It was relaxing?" Tatum offered. "I had the same sense. I mean, my shell when I found it again three months after I had thrown the two shells, was near the Statue of Liberty. North side along the Hudson river. Miss Enright, how good is she! I mean, there it was returned to me, on the very same spot! I picked it up, held it to my cheek, knowing this was a messenger for me from a far distance…. 'How far?' I'd asked."

"You did, Wow! That's the same puzzling question I asked my shell!" Greg laughs.

"What answer did the pink shell give?" Tatum was really jumping, so alive!

"The noise, beyond the waves, was clear. It answers: 'She is American. You did right by sending her back my pendant.. Listen up, I have something to reveal. Throwing me into the ocean, back into the current to

America. Soon you will hear from the voice of true love. With this one ear, I also reconnect with the one you sent home far away.'"

Greg said "At first I felt I was crazy. But you Tatum did something even more strange, getting it really moving you told me!?"

"Yes I did" says Tatum. "I found this black pearl and got it valued, checked. Miss Enright after all had told us, it's got code. When the second shell is thrown back, it records, sort of imprints who it's from and tracks that person…"

Greg smiles. "Really! That's so thrilling, it's amazing! So you got to see who I was. You even got a photo with my name and address!?"

"I did!" laughs Tatum. "And when I wrote you, in my old fashioned green ink, you replied, except you air-mailed back to me after a week!"

"We really found we have lots in common. And when we met, we had corresponded so many times" Tatum laughs.

"I came over after you invited me to Summer Camp!" says Greg.

"That was ten years ago.." Tatum smiles. "And finally I am here. My first visit! It is so romantic, England!"

Greg nods. "I recall you saying how you tied up all my letters with a rainbow of ribbons. Let's go back to Mersea and find some more Oyster shells!"

"Let's! Where you found our 'pink ears'!" laughs Tatum.

A DAY

The ant worried, was a whirligig of motion. Since first light had warmed his antennae eyes, the camp swarm was astir. Their worker nest was at the base-line of the tree, a species like the Canadian maple tree. It gave sustenance to many insects, including the ants.

Unknown to these ants, they provided a necessary function, with pollination of the flowers, giving fruits their glancing attention. The ants also prevented any foothold on its trunk by other predators.

In daylight, the ants were tyrannical fighters and merciless, unceasing workers. Globules of black treacle were extracted from the tree. These were carried in their sharp mandibles, to their nest below. Like beads of running perspiration they all teamed about; the ants, like an army marching as erratic clockwork, over the rough grey bark.

The sun cast dappling steady diffused light, spilling between the fronded branching leaves. As the bright time, the unhurried jungle hours passed, the damp and fetid earth floor spoke out. White tailed monkeys howled and customarily stoned with empty nut-shells an unwelcome hyena seeking shelter from the rising heat.

Beneath the canopy of the trees environs, the cicadas whirled on unerringly, as the almost soundless blue-turquoise and multicoloured life of humming-birds hung as azure filaments, showed sparkling in the low-hanging tones of daylight. As if awakening, the black wily python next to the tree, gripped the trees-vine and rubbed its side slowly, closely.

The ant was vexatious. It had wandered from the sticky seam of the treacly food. The light grew stronger, vivid to his quivering antennae. He was active and robotic; athletically speeding upwards, between the rufous, dank-grey bark.

A large grey moth skipped past his head, heading to the black, dank ground below. Nearby, parrots screeched and laughed, flying amongst fruit bearing trees. Their long beaks were tearing wastefully at many of the berries.

The ant had never been so high before in the one year of his life. His eyes were stronger, more penetrating it seemed, than his brothers. The indivisible, to many the daytime shadows of flying birds, were clearly seen by him. The crown of the tree he could view, even from the ground.

How he had longed to taste the fruit growing on other trees; the ripe blue and pink berries so loved by parakeets, wasps and the white-tailed monkeys.

Out of the corner of his antennae, when first the white pricking candle of dawn grew from beyond the east of their nest, he alone it seemed, could remember very early on in his life, many details of the jungle around the tree.

Today he was prepared, having fed-well the previous evening. The whole colony of workers were busy, for Springtime had arrived. The young were hatching and were hungry for ever more regurgitated heaps of syrup morsels. But the light drove him on. No longer the leaves shielded the Light from his primitive antennae eyes. No other drama or habit now hindered his marching determination.

He drummed his feet on the hot and shiny surfaces of the leaves. so high on top of the tree, reaching above the jungle. His black head looked out, probing the air. His young body quivered excitedly in the passing breeze and then his fragile drones' wings opened, both reflecting silver in the light, like razor blades, snapping apart.

Receptively catching on, he took to the air and was carried out, a minute insect helicopter, for whom destiny was moving. For founding other colonies, soaring far above the deep shading green of the jungle.

TUMBLING-OUT

Drew sees cross-winds. Wavering along high wires, they go skittering under dusty weed strewn lanes. He watches as leaves and stalks are lifting.. The cat shook all its paws..

'Shakey, shakey …'

Drew watched, mumbling 'Fishmonger!'.

He asks: 'How else..these bones…?'

Littering his backyards sparse kitchen garden on well raked tilth..Prints, impressed from the trails of dead fish; the leftover heads and tail suppers from his neighbours Tom cat, Mcgraw.

Gunther his father was just back from Norway. Drew couldn't speak or understand Norwegian. All he knew was a sea-fisher's life consisted of reeking oilskins, hauls of dry fish meal, bladderwrack and whale blubber. Gunther, as a seasoned Atlantic goer, walked on land with seagoing ambling strides.

An offering on Drews fifteenth birthday on their visit to a local husbandry store, Gunther brought his son these folded packets: crushed wedges of vegetables..like nostrums …

Drew took the carrots, planted rows. Gunther again stood beside his own short body; his dad so broad.. Drew edged away, along the narrow path, careful but still nudging him. Gunther is intent yet awkward, calm.

In his inner eye.. the wake of sea…while land is a league and more, far more.. A wake from harbouring. Terrifying the horizon, washing, foundering …..

'Your father…is gone..'

Gunther knows, feels and hears the battering torn storm clouds, thinking of presages, scarecrow watches. Crying screeching gulls, keepers of the light ship, from nightly dangers as the captain stays lashed to his wheel.

Terry, Drew's friend, jibes, 'Gunther is from Iceland. My dad says he's filled up with 'grog.' And, 'Vikings drink bulls blood..Are gung Ho!'

Drew runs from one end of the gym, side to side..The nearest to being ship mates, ship shaping..But only to muster and game-on, thumping along, running to shoot the basket with heavy rubber American balls …

Jib, tack..stay. Who has time to watch? Stay on board. Let go of castaways.

Gunther is out, zoned in icy spaces of glaciers and gravitas..toughening, absorbing him. Only the ocean's moving. Colliding with decked fastenings, nets, lanyards and steel hawsers.

Gotten clayfoot: Drew watched the birds pulling worms. On one side, the neat rows of threads marked the new lines of sowings. He had left these impressions after Gunther had stepped on the bare soil, It had meant more to Drew, setting here the horizon between his father and the under threading purpose..The near point..but far away, gone to sea and home…Sighting the mast of the trawler, disembarking as it hauls, disappearing aft..The stone ruck of the anchor soon lifting, fading noiselessly besides the diesel engines screwing its wake, passaging northwards…

Gunther looks at Drew. How the fish meal sticks..Wider are his nostrils ... 'Strange' Is he listening? My boy..He for the first asks 'Soon.' But there and again, 'So young ….'

When he was that age..Gardolf my father said 'We are Norse people..Die to go sea fishing. One's age is no matter. Brought up like silkies in brine …But my son…overfishing has lost herring fleets..Rocks cast us near..If we come nearer in land, we will be broken..ship wrecked.

Forging earth's better resilience. A new life means going back to earth..We who are fortune's fools, beyond pillage.

The cat came again. Drew kept both the cat and the annual weeds from encroaching. Mcgraw loves the smell of fishmeal and gets under the netting. Sometimes a caught sparrow is lucky. Drews sees the scare in the bird's eyes and relief. The knitted wings open, and are set flying free.

Mr Chivers asks: 'Are you coming to the show?'

Drew is taken aback, abashed that the village prizes new growers..Serious enough to enter. Drew is surprised, pleased when Mr Chivers visits. He bends over, brooding.

He says 'Never ever seen them so…Sure' He says 'These are sensational! He even holds up samples..How is this!?'

The vegetables are winners..Chivers says; 'Gunther is most proud!'

Drew shrugs..Gunther is late..will miss the village garden fete … 'I will display..win..perhaps!'

The morning arrives..Drew is up early. Drew goes to his garden allotment ..There is the scarecrow..But the garden is all thrown about. A deluge breaking the crop..A storm has gone through the ground overnight.. Drew runs all over checking, finding only wrack, the scuppers and wreckage and what is underneath..He recognises white fish skeletons..ship drownings and slippages …

Dried fronds and leaves are curling, rustling on the forsaken ground..Drew pinches himself, hearing a voice calling his name.

'At last, as a scullion …' The scarecrow's voice is Gunther's. 'Learn the language imparting, of Norse, my own father's..I'm gone down, lost and never returning.'

'Drew be unafraid. Weep not and dry those salty tears. Sea's cruel for those unprepared. To you far away I came on the wind. The sea always draws so near. Gunther's ready. Next season: Till and hoe, diligently. Hereafter life's for the both of us!We'll harvest earth's homecoming, growing a new garden.'

HELIUM LIFT OFF

Some people have all the luck, getting enviable presents. Tarquin Benadale had his coming late. Grubs was his friend. Except things got sticky. Like they were taking over.

He had them from the garden, snails crawling up the bedroom walls. Ones with scary eyes, droning. As evening wore on, rattling and talking; yes talking! About aliens and gossip, the neighbours and political things and all..

It was crazy and it sucked. 'Cos nobody would believe him and this made him feel even madder. But more importantly though, they stayed around. The bugs gave him a gift: Of synesthesia, seeing with green eyes. Yes, green. Glowing in the dark.'

The largest bug was called Mortrum. With a glittering mouth, it spoke only as it grew dark. Tarquin tended to sit in the corner of his room, with his hands cupped around his ears. Attentive to every chaffed sound, interpreting the sounds into words.

"Men suck!" Mortrum signalled. "They haven't got a clue! Really they are the subsoil species. You see we connect up with the bigger picture."

Tarquin offered quizzically, "It's your antennae isn't it?"

Mortrum demurred, "Well only partly. Your so-called attitude to alien life is your shutdown defense. The realities are more tertiary; we see with odour spectrums. Linking us to other invisible, but near living islands."

Mortrum paused, adding "Don't be afraid: you are not different. All men are parasites to aliens. And more particularly insects!"

It was no dream. The room was getting bigger. Tarquin was not merely fascinated by the bugs, but was being absorbed by them. "Biological knowledge" he thought. "Why yes, they pupate. Are voracious eaters, absorbing mainly cellulose.

A kind of initiating ceremony, it was also cross-fertilising into their species. He knew they had overwhelming power over his intelligence. It fascinated him.

For as Mortrum said, "You are the first Tarquin. I can instruct you from our highest source in 'Galactia H', or to you, by the Grand Hardwick Triggers. Tarquin shall remain as a man. Yet shall operate with far more extreme gifts and forms. Having a greater being than we have, living as an alien. Gifted to fly and see with bugging life."

For a long time things stayed quiet. Tarquins' was a one parent household. Frank Roper, his dad, ran a light holding of twenty-thousand cattle. Plus an oil well from two stations in the north and south. Out on the prairie all day, Frank directed Galvia, his oil rep, to find Tarquin a tutor.

Tarquin was well prepared. Mortrum had sent messengers out in advance, attaching chemical sensors to the candidates skin. One Georgio Millada ended up driving off a cliff. The second, Kruger Rhienfold ran an insecticide spray company down in Detroit. He got stung to death by killer bees.

Professor Mindfeld was luckier. Tarquin revealed to him how he had found deposits or pockets of helium. In two places fifteen and twenty miles from the farm. This thankfully, kept him busy.

The grubs had been busy, especially at night. Another world was opening up to Tarquin. Not only was there drinking below, but the rooftop became noisy and very busy too. Mortrum still slithered about, but had grown horns and legs. Reminding Tarquin of the Greek figure, the Minotaur.

The great thing was the tunnels he traveled about under the floor. They carried ships and cargoes of aliens and were mostly all friendly. 'So above, so below.' It seemed they were big to him. Flying as though by electricity. But in scale to the house, perhaps they were indeed microscopic in size.

Professor Mindfeld got Tarquin busy with prospecting. He said "Once we've gotten over extraction, we'll get down to some serious studies. For now Tarquin, we're needing to do real estate business. We need dogs, lots of them too."

"Why?" said Tarquin. Mindfeld wasn't used to explaining anything, only giving out orders. He scratched his head. He bit his lip, stopping the crunch word 'stupid', only because Frank was his boss.

"Dogs" he offered, can smell helium, not us humans. It's quite alien.

Dogs have E.S.P. Extra noses or spectrums."

At home, Mortrum got the biggest bugs. Now all changed into snoopy doggy dogs and they filled up five trucks.

The dogs got right into it, yet were wary of this noxious gas. It made the dog yap too much after all. For men, it brought the fullest grown to tears.

The Professor said "Yes, it's a primitive commodity, useful for a cheap civil flying resource. We are on the verge of bringing back cheap air balloons for trans-globalisation."

Other instructions had been given to the dogs. Grand Hardwick Triggers saw an opportunity to control these flights from inside. Tarquin saw to it. All the dogs were co-opted out to field workers and everyone wore named owner badges. Essential green stickers. By this way, everybody changed allegiance to the Grand Plan.

Professor Mindfeld felt the hairs on his neck stiffen, recognising the smell of helium. He was unaware that his eyes glowed green in the dark.

Frank Roper's dog Mutton Jeff had a specialkind of relationship with his owner. Firstly, of mutual respect for the tidbits of meat and secondly, the detestation of natural bugs. Mutton Jeff snapped at and saw off any territory threats. Both to his beloved dogs and that was for miles around. He was a busy dog.

Frank often had bloodshot eyes arguing with Tarquin and everybody else for that matter against the reality of UFO's, or extreme existence of alien's.

"There really is son, nothing of the kind on this Earth. I'll kill you if you just mention such a thing. I'm busy now. Don't call me. Buzz up the Professor. I'm swathing hay for my cattle."

The coyote watched the trailer pass him a hundred, then three hundred times. Frank had seen him, despite the hypnotic work, feeding the swathed hay binding into the machine drum. The coyote bided his time. He knew the works would get stuck. Often the machine driver got tired or lazy.

Greedy to finish and overfilled the machine. Mortrum had done his work well; the oil workers had all been turned into mice. The coyote leapt and lunged. There was almost too much food. He was very strong. It had been easy catching Mutton Jeff. He had grown too inquisitive, leaping into the path of the binder as he followed him.

Frank had been stopped by the screaming. As he worked to free the bale, the coyote reached into the cab, turning the binder back on. Frank too quickly got drawn in. His head lashed up against the iron spindles. Turning to face the green eyes of the hungry coyote, grinning up at him.

'The empty box of his toy balloon was all that was left' read the Missouri Times banner. Out across the plain, a thick dark pallor from the gas was lit only by white vans raking burning fires. As a precaution, the army had razed the place to the ground.

'Was there a cover-up?' ran the article. 'What happened to the strange cigar-shaped planes seen flying into the night skies over the farm?

How did Frank Roper die?'

It continued, 'there may soon be answers to this riddle. His son Tarquin is returning from abroad and of course has claims on the farm. Here is a copy of his fax.' Reading: 'he breeds a super bug to clean up all the helium. A round-up man.'

THE RIVER DEBEN

The Deben river in view at Woodbridge at low tide. I see the brown slimy shining soft replenishing mud with a seam of streaming water running in-flowing from the ebb tide returning. A barren trickling bird-calling place on a bright early morning.

The thin seaweed is sizzling amidst the swish of outflows. Canadian geese, counted 55 rise slowly waddling up the far flats like an anciently clan-like congregation the farthest grouping, steering toward the farthest shoreline: a bank of grass below the far trees on the crest of the horizon.

The boats: yachts of several sizes have turned in the current, now facing west. Two pairs of swans pass them, drinking serenely and slowly, dipping their curling necks, drinking the water and preening. Their forms reflected, dropping white feathers into the languid water. Farther upstream a heron sentinel like, stands and mechanically moves, resuming his stark firm poise watchfully.

Repetitive as a croaking frog, a lone duck is driven by five approaching swans from midstream onto the flats. A single goose also leaves the water, followed by the mate of another, finding the mud deep, as both purposefully yet quickly march up east, past where I sit. The seagulls fly indolently, dropping down to prick at the river's edge before soaring away again; turning up into the air, rising and beating along the air.

The river curves, broken by the encroaching mud banks. A playful black crow stands on a bench seat, insistently taunting at the river birds before flying northwards, settling on to a beached motorboats prow. It continues calling out, bobbing its head, it's voice harsh and repetitive. A swan, tossing and bathing it's puffed out feathers in midstream, motions replying.

The heron has stepped out onto an old slipway, his footsteps stitching up again in methodical rhythm to the water and again slowly, feet enter the shallows. Two oystercatchers flick at the mud, their beaks like needles darting forwards, persistently reaching for food. One leaves, flying out. The wings, white flickering, are in a contrasting pattern against the flat black shadows of the calm waters. Across the far bank it flies, lifting above tall hedges, heading over the banking hills marking Sutton Hoo. The sandy fields are presently growing beet and maize below the horizon of Scots pine woodland.

Three green male mallards soar past, chasing a single hen, calling once, twice again. The geese are turning round, the gaggle in unison are trumpeting together; their fat brown bodies like horn pipes waddling down towards the river; vocal, flat footed on the mud.

The sky is clear but for a plane's vapour trail. Before me, the geese hear the train coming into the station. The metal squeaks, the locomotive's body halting briefly before the clanking of wheels rolling the metal stock forwards out of the yard, pulsing and then quickening towards Ipswich. The geese move away too, walking further up, the bank disturbed temporally by the mechanical noises. Looking south-east far away, a heat haze pales the colours of the fields patchwork, turning blue-gray the parsley shaped trees like smoke in the far distance.

A swan flicks it's wings like paddles going south, taking off and flies but not going far up, curving a few hundred yards before sinking down to the water again. There's another pulse, an oarsman passes, sculling north in midstream, leaving a long trail like hair threading the water, breaking the film of the surface, effortless in steady slow movement. Above, a flecking group of pigeons wheels and climbs as one, clustered together as bees. They move and soar quickly becoming faint to the eye, then invisible.

Bubbles drift, pricking the passage of the rower. Another joins him far to the left, tacking to his moored white yacht. Five young ducks sit like buoys, softly sliding and bleating in the water. The great group of brown coloured Canadian geese have joined them, separating the far bank like a flotilla of regal Elizabeth warships, threading north in a long elegant train. Their forms are clearly silhouetted on the silvery brown river's surface. Floating together, they sail on purposefully with the drifting tide below the Tide Mills basin.

A gull rises above them, talking and flying, as if frustrated by this clamour, commotion…A number of the geese have walked again onto the midstream mud flats, others turn and enter into the river's central stream as they meet and rise up onto the far bank. Black breakers of rotten wood, river groins boundary the far shore line.

I hear a woman pass, talking to her golden retriever and black labrador: "I think we'll have to go further along." She smiles at me in her blue shorts. The dogs pant and watch her playfully as they run before her along the near footpath. The haze is lifting.

The man in the schooner has set his red sail, awaiting the rising tide. A far buoy is winking, lifting with the waters. Several ducks are very talkative and playful in the water. People are passing, strolling out. Before me, from left to right, I count five filing ducklings in a line, eagerly foraging on the near mud with their mother paddling with them, searching for bills of food.

Their father joins them. I count six now. Their noisy beaks make swishing, dribbling and scooping sounds. They're quick and always run ahead of their parents; between them walks a slower chick.

Walking in unison, trumpeting geese edge away from the river base and tremor along the thin reedy water, threading low. Like a battlefield, its cutting is vied by cormorants, their shadows echoing. The fleet of river boats are all stranded; amateur holiday riggers are docked by the retreating tide. The water's wake is drawn away and the hazy air hangs beyond on the hills.

Like South American pan-pipes, flying sandpipers blow short entreaties on the rising heat and oozing mud. The chocolate mud mired swathes are camouflaged with khaki seaweed. Swans preen themselves upon the mill-pond pools, each as turning feathers, drifting and dreaming. In the warmth of the sun, some swans are opening their lotus-like wings, while others are closed up, their necks sleeping.

Propellers lie idle behind their keels. There is no man navigating or preparing their ships for sail

. On the farther shore, the sand conceals black shiny fossils of shark teeth. Amber and samphire, rose-bay willow and a far spreading stain of flowering red sorrel is broken by meadowsweet's satin white sashes.

Old ropes are rotting in the lanyards, the silences stirred by the recoil of rook scarers. The weir of the Tide Mill is near; the old six-penny ferry ride is discernible by a tank track on the far river side. Verdant greenery of trees and wild hedges are cleaved by the wide waters flowing on through them.

'Zip-zoo, zo, zo, zi, zo, zip, zip, zip zoo' sings two passing grey legs in the river, going up stream. The tide is down, yet rises as the cloud glows, blurs with the warming sun.

The heron waits patiently like a metal statue in the north near riverside, pointy like a spear, sharp eyed. He is watching the rings of fish fingers point, opening their ringing air-holes. Rag worms blow in the mud like grass casts. Slow moving are the stagnant waters, slimier than the filmy grease of the lapped mud of the rivers undercurrent and underbelly.

Fishes run through oily weeds fleshing out, creeping apace - wandering forwards into broadening ringing space. The sky falls upon the waters surface, merging light with the green opal and sullen grey.

Wide weaving, a swallow rolls about the air - incessant as the river cleaves onward. 'Rebel', 'Kiri' and 'Tomboy'. With other indecipherable boats names are moored, shelved above the tide line. Standing idly, large and small crafts with rudders immured as icebergs, wait for tar and fouling in the chandlers yards.

A black swan sits by a water pipe outflow, it's neck curved into itself like a handle, preening its chest plumes. Preening around it are other white swans. Some, eighteen in number, are cruising over from the far bank.

In the still soothing light of evening, an army task force helicopter clips the trees over the horizon eastwards, turning round and round over Woodbridge air base. The air pulsates with a thunderous threshing noise. Beating in time are wind-jams of wires clipping, ticking against the aluminium sail poles.

Hungrily the gulls scour the rivers edge and along the embankment pathway for some morsels Ozone, mixed with salt, the soft movement of the air twists the wild barley tares and spiky green spinach. Contrasting with this plain stern concrete tide wall, the far south rolls away with unspoilt verdure.

Endless is the edge of slime coated far bank rubbed tidally to soft crumbling soil, topped over with tufted marram grass. Beyond the white feathery reed beds, a pinioned headdress conceals the ferry man's broken grey wooden hut. Further back, fields rise on a higher plain, half separated in the potato crops dark green. The other half has yellow grasses on sandy soil.

This river vista is a sunny place: calmly reflective as a sky mirror in the waters. Nine single canoeists outflank the swan party, turning out from the youth club, keeping line rhythmically with their paddling in mid-channel. The boys chatter with gusto. Like the swans, they move in a similar harmonious pattern, drawn to the ambient leisure of the quickening waters.

The seaweed tossed smell assails the nasal sense, washed and dissolved here by oceanic flows …darting swallows fly close to the wrinkled waters surface with white underbellies, lifting and clipping above black shining waters, feeding and passing, scooping up insects.

Amidst the wastes the course's continuing currents flow on naturally, as natural as breathing. Languorous and essential, plastic buoys sit with harboured caskets of fettered boats, captured at entrances to the river's movement and passageways.

Hooded and on one leg, numerous geese stand resting on the far river side. Four swans are swimming out this morning, turning. A black swan swims behind. One swan uncurls away from the others, flowing downstream, following the others going with the running-out tide. The sky is broken up. The clouds, in an all smoky panoply of dancing formations and slow-scything free-forms, are brightly milky in colour. The foreground is pea-green, with wig-shaped clumps of seaweed littering the shingly mud.

Looking south over to Waldringfield, the low fields appear to bar the river course, turning it into a bay. Again, with the tide low, depleted of waters, one lone man rows, struggling against the reducing tide. Getting out, he pulls the boat onto the mud, moored with a red buoy to a fixed line.

All the swans are resting. One is asleep on the water, so still it might have died. Staggering strangely, waddling drunkenly, the swans each awaken, leaving the bank, stepping down from side to side slowly. Lifting their webbed feet awkwardly out from the mud, each enters gracefully into the easeful waters. Over the waters, a race is on, a thanksgiving party of geese are running to catch up with the gathered geese crowding on the shoreline.

A rower pauses., talking to another man silhouetted far off, heaving and slow forking into the cloying mud. He lifts and parts, weighing each portion, searching for rag worms. The rower drifts on, parting his oars. He too stops and moors his boat downstream, hauling it from the waters. Carrying a bucket and fork, he walks a few paces searching, then turns back. He begins to dig next to the edge of the water, turning ponderously the blackish-slimy mud slowly for eels and worms. Then moving on, he drops a small object into the can. Near geese are disturbed by this black-legging figure; they turn, marching up the shoreline, again stopping safely a few yards south.

A man in red overalls punts away after working on the shore. With one oar in his turquoise coloured boat he stands, edging along ... moving out with the current, the cool westerly breeze catching him, passing a cormorant standing with widespread stretching wings.

Down river, the clouds have darkened the water, while the sun catching a yellow field of rape grasses, fusing temporally the river's slate-grey colours. White and blue the sky filters, watering the banks of brown merged with green.

GALLAVANTINGS

'Big wrists, huge hearts.' "I come from a long line of lasooists", Jack our hero blurted. 'Of all trades' most saw him as a modern designer dog.

Carrier of wedges, whips, mountain pitons. Music played upon his lips.

He would slide in like sugar into a cake, between lonely meetings. A catalyst between vitriol curmudgeon parties. Star turn at sparring or blood sports. A heckler amidst fighters.

The repartee cut ice and quickened the savage breast. Soothing the blistered mouth in those years of Jack Moragee. Travelling in his barge and van. He has the snout of a ferret, daily running his whippets.

Behind the curtain: retinues of foxes, cockerels and bandwagons of animals. Theatre's artifices, wands, and cloaks. Jack too wore masks. He struck out, season after season across the countryside. Between haunts of fairs, circuses and haulier meetings. Down slow canals. The wayfarer at Gypsy sites: he welded up cars and exchanged for pigeon and partridge's eggs.

There were duels under the moon with razor blades dancing. At the new moon, the sound of Mexican violins and the wailing of dogs echoing over tin roofs. The wagon rolled: the fullness of winning. Driving away bullion. Bales of satins. Flying feathers along the dusty roads.

Some spoke of Jack's green hands. Others, his black palms, after long periods of wayfaring. Those long disappearances from out their lives.

"I follow my heart" was his retort, bemused by the treacheries and confusions of the modern highway. Often, he would say "What music I hear!" Or, "Why is there such din or discordance, the idle rattling of drums, like war after battles?"

Crowds' voices lingered in his heart; wayfarers conversations stuck in cul-de-sacs. Or at junctions of ghost towns.

"While I ", he said "am bemused, rattle through them. Asking and blinking. There is no meanness here, only arcades of golden lights. Neon's assuming bright passages".

Once he came again to Count Moulwins house, at the base of the Pertwesyn mountains. Indeed, the large place was cut from the rock and its halls, embedded far back, were made from that stone.

Count Moulwin had made it all himself.

"My father was a bird catcher". He had once confided in Jack.

"For the miners in these parts you understand. I was brought up to explore these caverns. I found gold. Yet more importantly, I made myself work. And carving here I made my home, my fortune. My visitors come to live here"

He guffawed; "The whole house at first looked like slate but was all gleaming as if it was open at night!"

'A huge window to the stars' thought Jack. In fact it was polished as a mirror. But here there was another difference: it was a tunnel to the other world.

"I am lifted up here," said the Count.

"It's very wonderful!" agreed Jack. They spent days being amused, just walking around the house. For as they entered the huge apartments, they opened into outdoors park ways, And the grey light brightened.

Upon the hill sides they were joined by many lively people, ambling leisurely.

At the heart of the house a fire burnt and singers sat about on horses, after long journeys. Jack knew many and was amused at them riding to and fro.

Retinues of horses, hawkers leaping dogs and flaming fire-eaters sported too. The incandescent light and laughter rolled across the plains and rang from the sides of the mountain.

Count Moulwin said "I have built a mill here. Once there was only sand; music wrote this place. The rivers here are as rich as milk and I have been given so many riches, honey and charms aplenty. As you see: here I am brought into a rich country! A tapestry of a charmed life, flowing like a river past my door."

Jack was always a foundry maker. "I work in melted metals from mountain ores. There is work to be done."

The Count spoke with gleaming eyes. He had a special way with him; of flying and talking to birds. Count Moulwin had their pact and patronage. Jack understood this.

The Count said "make me living creatures out of their music. I am one with their invisible life: yet I am sad. I must give them their dreams. Breathe fire into their passing whispers. Gather me some here."

So it was. Jack climbed the mountain. He found the bare rock face hard going at first. The rock was cold and remote and the vast empty plateaus, dizzying and lonely.

Count Moulwin had turned his back on Jack, saying "go for forty days and nights. Learn alone the voices of these great peaks. Hear the mewing of the eagles and kites. Know the ways of carrion and the weeping of flesh. Steal in your heart the loss and lose your way. Then gather it all back to me, the music of its life."

It was in the beginning Jack met Cronx, the flesh eater who admonished him, saying "Jack yet I fly, be still. We, the elemental ice spirits in the belly of the mountain ranges also have waited for your visit in the black space. At the rising red Moon's centre at our shoulder. We dart ice pinions, brightening down the sky before morning. Shouting thunder in the night!"

He paused, "Now Jack, taking the inspiring energy of our fire, be crowned.

Your second head anointed with power, return home to the Count. From out of the Earth, man is fashioned. As flame is remade. Now is the time of unfolding our terrain. The face of spirit living."

When Jack got home he found the Count had gone. So too had the house closed up. Jack twisted the key into his van and took to the road. Yet in his minds' eye gleamed a new light. And from his galavantings something had come good. Never one to idle, Jack was not one to doubt.

The dark house he left behind stood undisturbed. That pleased him enormously. Jack looked behind. A golden white river ran, shining in his mirror.. Big black birds rolled across the horizon and silver light glistened from the sky.

BROOK FARM

Juggan got into a gunfight that early morning, cleaning out Brook Farm at Shottisham.

"For all your work." His Aunt Maggie met him at his Uncle Shamish's garage the previous morning. Shamish was away up at Holt on business, but left instructions. "I've got three models in, two are classics. Red upholstered E-Jaguars. I want him to have one. The farm is prospering from his hard labours."

Juggan's drove Maggie down to Aldeburgh in the newest Jag and they had lunch at the Brudenell Hotel.

Juggan's father left him only one item, an A P Waffen-Spanau Luger. Somehow he had been allowed as a keepsake after his capture in '44: spending time first at Hollesley Bay, then at Holt penitentiary on the Norfolk coast.

Juggan remembers his father cleaning the gun, then throwing it across the room.

"You keep it!"

Juggan pulled it out of the grate before the fire consumed it. Only now, as he drew it and pulled the trigger did it work; the old boar Tummel had gone frenzied - bashing all about the pig's pen - madly protecting Bertha and her eight piglets.

All 360 Kilos of this large black pig, ran forwards at Juggan, flagrantly berserk! The squealing beast lunged at Juggan's head as he'd overhung the pen, watching Tummel's might.

The boar rose to the top and smashed straight through, flinging him over. Juggan flew crashing down, beyond the frenzied boar down into the acrid straw strewn litter. Mud streamed all over him. Despite his excluding breath and body blow, Juggan rummaged, drawing out his weapon.

Flicking off the safety catch, Juggan aimed as Tummel turned round. The gun fired, shooting bright fire piercing the tumult. Instantly, Tummel's tiny bogey black eyes screw up. His champing jaws bristle enraged.

The bullet struck! Instantly Tummel stampeding forwards stopped. Going down he swerves and upends. His ghoul, bludgeoned skull recoils losing his trotters. His legs slipping gives out with a vestigial squall. Tummel is snorting as his blood blandishes, and thrashes. Spilt flesh collides through splashing mud.

The piglets first ran about, then all in pitching squeals run to the far end of the pen. Bertha got straight up. She seemed totally unaware of Juggan, lumbering past him to Tummel, lying stone dead. She licked first Tummel's fallen ears; her muzzle shuffled forwards pouting and tasted the offal. The compound's a black rack. Silence quickens to sounds of maws and mashing.

Bertha is crunching and chomping. Guts still steam, the brown slime of the straw had been churned, chimed over. Groats and off-yellow turnips spill over the gouging cuts. Tummel's flesh bursts open, turning into viands.

Swiftly Juggan rose, leaped over the sides of the pig compound. Inwardly Juggan's stomach revolts. He lands, squats with palpable anguish, tasting putrid panic. In his hands is an astringent; cold steel brings compassion, solace.

Meyer, his father before dying, opens up his bedside drawer, takes out and hands Juggan a black portmanteau.

He says "I'm wanting you to have these, there is a clip of bullets. Only at the last moment use them, but never in anger - promise me! If you do - remember this. A gun, when fired teaches you what you kill, respect. You live after and must save good thoughts. Learn never to do it again.

Destruction must always be wasteful. Do not harbour pride - it's no thrill!"

BLACK CAYMAN EGWAH

Da Monto lived near New Orleans in the swamps. While Soto his wife wasn't keen on monster crayfish or on hunting giant black Cayman alligator's - Da Monto and his two son's Rafi and Delgo loved fishing. They had a pen-zoo at home all of their own. Soto salts the fish and sings the blues in bars.

The swamps has private islands all across the coastal edges. A green sea-dragon lives there, spitting yellow spumes beyond the Sargasso sea. During daytime, Da Monto sells hotdogs, rum breezers, hot-snake cookies, down-town from his barrow in Louisiana. At night, he's Brigand Da Monto, on board his galleon named Luisha and takes adventurers to join with other pirates and sea-goers.

Rafi is the oldest son of Soto, brought up by pirate Captain Razu wearing a huge red beard. Carrying six gold cutlasses in his belt, he never argues but laughs or loudly shouts out his orders. "Captain Razu is my second father, before Da Monto met Soto "says Rafi. "I stay with both of these men."

In fact Captain Razu often sails away on marauding grappling parties. Mostly, the Captain stays in his big tank, besotted with his green parrots, basking sharks and snub-nosed porpoises.

Delgo goes out alone on early mornings, driving the sea-raft out far across the swamps and gathers pelican and turtle eggs. Shooting the rapids, he then dares at beating the Cayman, lying in wait to snap his boat as it passes around their powerful steel-trap jaws. Further-on, as the tall ships of the pirates appear in the misty horizons, the villages on stilts, dwellings of Borrio Indians, come out of their houses to barter with Delgo.

The elder Chief Zce sits before him, surrounded by all the tribesmen. "This island is floating upon the Sargasso ", he reminds Delgo. "We are pearl fishers. Our queen is the Green Dragon. She has a daughter. Go visit her." He added, "But be warned. The jade gates are locked. Hungry and angry spotted jaguars run right around the arcing parameter of the Green Dragon's island. No King or Pirate has ever set foot here into the Green Dragon's sanctuary."

Chief Zce had one gift for Delgo, a golden egg. "Take this, it is all she craves..The Green Dragon shall bear a son."

On returning across the swamps, a great storm arose. A giant sized Cayman named Egwah, snapped at Delgo's raft. The first snap sent the raft up into the air! The second snap snapped it into two and Delgo was sent flying. In his rucksack was the golden egg and all the other eggs, from albatrosses, pelicans and the turtles. All, together with Delgo, fell into the open mouth of the Cayman, who quickly disappeared into the inky sea.

That night, the giant sized black Caiman Egwah met with his army. "This Green Dragon has found favour with Chief Zce. She, in return for a golden egg, offers her daughter's hand. As you know, long ago, in the mists of our time, I was to marry the Green Dragon…"

"Yes, Yes, Yes' ', the army of Cayman all roared out. "That was before these islands arose, or Pirates drove us under the swamps" they all chorused.

Egwah snarled, "Enough, you meddling 'gators! I want what is mine. I have in my safe warm belly -It Aches So…!!!"

Edgware stopped to rub his stomach. Green coloured tears of renown Cayman's vexation rolled down his purple cheeks. "The golden egg, it is here."

Egwah pointed to his sagging stomach. His faded red leather stomacher, covering his chest, had green seaweed fronds sewn tightly, holding the extra weight crammed there-in.

"My own son Egwah minor..and the young Wippa-Snappa - is Alive-Oh…Delgo! I have a plan! Listen-Up!!!", demanded Egwah.

The army of 'gators keenly stirred. Their tails curled and fell, as the inched forwards eagerly. Egwah said, "I shall go to Da Monto tonight to summon-up the pirates!"

All the 'gators all immediately laughed. So impressed and pleased were they for Egwah, they answered back, "That is Our Plan, Yes, Yes, Yes!"

Da Monto was asleep, gently rocking in his hammock. Up rose into the holding pool, the black snapping form of Egwah the Cayman. Waters foamed and thrashed and wildly flew.

"Hey What!" Exclaimed Da Monto, turning round. "Whah, By Gorror, Huh! You …Cayman…Egwah!!! What brings you here?!"

Egwah lay back, still now in the pool. The green pond weed settled back steadying below his bright black sharp eyes.

"You Pirate!", levelled Egwah. Have you lost somebody Ken? Know and care about this!" hissed Egwah.

"I have", he paused, smacking together his jaws. "With me, my prisoner, your son Delgo! As a favour, you can have him back alive or dead. What would you prefer?"

Da Monto shook his fist, reaching for his cutlass, then dropped his hand. "What do you want, Egwah? I want Delgo Alive of course!"

Egwah said, "Gadzooks! What splendid sense you have! You pirates have powers - Use them! Delgo shall return sad. But you firstly must open the gates of the Green Dragon. Delgo has been invited to take the Green Dragon's own daughter's hand..and..well, she the Green Dragon has to reckon with me. She has my own son!"

Egwah's head sank..murmuring, "I must marry her again!"

The Indian Pearl fishers met with Da Monto and Soto. Outward bound in the Luisha Galleon they sailed. Meeting with Captain Razu, five Pearl fishers carried with them the Green Dragon's message. "Her consolation", they revealed "Is Egwah: he has made moves, with offerings to Chief Zce."

The Pearl fishers had rewards of pearls and piled high treasures Egwah had hoarded. They were shared out to Chief Zce, the Green Dragon and Captain Razu. The Pearl fishers then returned, bringing a message to Egwah.

"I have waited for you Egwah, now I open my island to him."

Delgo was set free and met the Green Dragon's daughter. The Green Dragon was very thrilled." This is a time for all Pirates and Islanders to come together. Let us celebrate." She added, "My son, soon my son shall be hatched!"

BUTCHERS FIRESIDE

Mr Rutter yawned as Tobbit, his ample sized ginger cat plucked and sank deeper into his lap. The master was toasting his feet in front of the grate of a roaring stove-fire, as was his practise at the start of the evening, an hour after the working day, at his home. And just now, he had begun to doze.

The butchering trade wasn't easy, standing all day long, littering the floor with the fresh supply of birch shavings, splitting the beef sirloins, sharpening the knives and waiting and serving at the till. These were merely a sample of his routine pursuits.

Arnold, his dutiful assistant, usually helped with the routine business of miscellaneous butchering work but had been laid off with hepatitis jaundice. Mr Rutter had a busy day.

Worst of all, he recalled how he had carelessly overlooked clearing up the shop's abattoir, whilst collecting the Managers package of beef and onion sausages. He had returned back to the shop after luncheon and he had slipped and hit his right shoulder.

Today, there had been no parsley and sage stuffing, but he was grateful for the plastic parsley; edging the window dishes it did so pleasingly.

How his bruised shoulder ached, especially in the evenings; always the little worries, he thought.

Mr Rutter pinched up his toes again, as his usually sensitive hearing tracked a muzzy blowfly wandering willy-niLly above him, across the ceiling. The flaring logs spat and crackled, as the heat wafted out and stuck his grey flannel trousers onto his legs.

Little nervous age lines, creased across his shining pink forehead, pricked also now by a damp and rosy sheen of heat. His big hands, like red shining industrial gloves, gave in to imponderable leaden tiredness; soon they were hanging easily over the sides of his armchair.

His figure breathed heavily, and sponge-like; the steady compressions of his diaphragm, wheezily disappeared downwards, towards his rounded stomach, onwards meeting his still and out-spread legs.

The room leapt with yellow Light from the flames flaring about, all glimmering, flickering and dancing against the deepening gloaming.

Just now Mr Rutter was asleep, dreaming of a rather outsized carcass and he was basting it and turning it slowly on a spit; the flesh was roasting well.

A thought crossed his somnolent mind, with some faint annoyance, that several of his regular customers were present at the barbecue. The point of his concern was he really doubted if they had been invited and was perturbed by their forceful insistence at being served. Like cattle at a trough, they collectively thrust themselves forward, pushing upwards at him, their empty white plates.

On trying the meat and touching the smooth, untextured moistened flesh, he was startled by the sudden and perplexing sound of a braying ass, intermingled with the rather piteous noises of a lamb or rabbit bleating.

To Mr Rutter, looking again at his patrons, each looked more familiar to him; they also had curiously assumed the forms and faces of rams. Their butting horns were menacing him. The meat tasted rather under-done, as he sliced himself off a sliver from the roast; he was very hungry.

Just now Mr Rutter was asleep, dreaming of a rather outsized carcass and he was basting it and turning it slowly on a spit; the flesh was roasting well.

A thought crossed his somnolent mind, with some faint annoyance, that several of his regular customers were present at the barbecue. The point of his concern was he really doubted if they had been invited and was perturbed by their forceful insistence at being served.

Like cattle at a trough, they collectively thrust themselves forward, pushing upwards at him, their empty white plates.

On trying the meat and touching the smooth, untextured moistened flesh, he was startled by the sudden and perplexing sound of a braying ass, intermingled with the rather piteous noises of a lamb or rabbit bleating.

To Mr Rutter, looking again at his patrons, each looked more familiar to him; they also had curiously assumed the forms and faces of rams. Their butting horns were menacing him. The meat tasted rather under-done, as he sliced himself off a sliver from the roast; he was very hungry.

Another queer and instinctive idea crossed his mind. "I have become a ram", and he reached up and touched his own head. Instantly he felt a bony excrescence protruding there, the unmistakable substance of animal horns.

He felt his heart, usually as buoyant as spring-water and as well-timed as a crystal, now as leaden and clotted as cold marble. Impatiently, he raked his cloven hooves in the wet mud and flicked his knotted tail. The other animals with steamy nostrils, nuzzled up to him, closer now. Their pained rolling eyes red and white glinting.

Their bodies showed the aggressive power of steam engines. Instinctively, he turned to the meadow grass and then chewed his fill.

The night-scented stocks outside the open window emitted their delicate perfume clearly into the butchers' room and lessened the odours from his fireside slippers, toasting up beside the stove. The cat had fallen asleep but stirred again as Mr Rutters clock chimed out six quick notes: its bell ringing loudly in his undisturbed lounge. Again Tobbit, rallied by the fading echoes of the clock, also answered a deeper, more urgent call, the rumbling noise of his empty feline stomach.

A lone and wary fat mouse became Tobbit's unfortunate victim, for whom the hour of six had also proven significant, if not cruelly unkind. The master would be having his meal later than usual and tonight's meal, when prepared, would probably be served-up cold!

THE BLINDMAN AND DOVE

Summer had arrived for the family of the doves. Their first Summer for the new-born was borne out from the elm tree, and the feathers, with their downy coverings tautened and grew shining. And directly they were coherently of one shape, they flew skyward, flying quicker than the clouds and more sensible than the lonely stars or the gallant zephyr lightning.

The trusting nest, the parents had carefully placed between vee-shaped twigs, upon the masthead of the tallest elms. As tall pillars, these stood, stony trunks solemnly swaying responsible in their steely charge, toward the broody mother dove and her yet sleeping hatchlings.

The two doves had courted twin-like in love, and Spring gave of itself. The opening flowers bore colourful beatitudes while the gambolling lambs played, and the bees embroidered the tuneful hues of balmy peaceful days.

And so renewed, the wooing white doves saw how life was abundantly alive; quietly peaceful they became, cooing and crooning toward their awakening life. On their branches they gave prayers and the eggs continued to grow from the ochre of the night, towards the crystalline laughing day.

How the free stairways of the air and sky ran hitherward into the sun-breathing day! The bird's wings flew, tossed to all the far corners, as the snail and mole, with the periwinkle and stones, all cast wide their dreams.

And the blind man proffered in his finding, learning to exact his kindness upon a dove, fallen from the sky with one broken wing. The man had lost his sight very early and when young, his mother had told him vivid stories. During the quiet moments of the day, he recited poems to himself.

Often the doves, cooing softly above him, soothed his heart. They sang in the trees, close to his cottage. And he would gently rock himself to sleep in the bottom of his boat, lying on the edge of the slow-flowing river.

He would dream and sometimes it was of a fortress. He would stand as a knight in armour at the bottom of a hill, looking up at it. On other occasions, he dreamed of a cherry tree, split in the middle, yet fully in blossom. Then before him, in his dream, he stumbled across a head of stone, buried up to its neck in the sand. Carrion surrounded it, picking up beetles and pecking at the eyes of the stone head.

And he dreamed of a caravanserai, leaving upon a long journey. The children were all smiling and sat upon the wagons, which were all piled up with belongings. So content to be gone, they invited him to go with them.

He would awaken to the evening sounds of the blue fronded palm leaves, rustling with a quiet and soothing noise against themselves, knocking the bow-sides of his boat. The dove now, resting on his lap, with a splintered wing, was regaining its strength for freedom again. The man knew in his mind's eye, that it would not be long before he would place this dove in his out-stretched palms, open under the sky, And before them, the welcoming land lay open and alive.

A DOG'S LIFE

"Carnivores are hunters, large meat eaters, killing prey only for survival." The teacher, Miss Tatlin, insistently under-lined the point. "For man, it is quite unethical. Cannibalism threatens the species.."

The pig squealed in his ear 'a dream, a nightmare? Johnny Smith had interrupted, "But Miss, my father eats bacon every morning for breakfast. "The class burst into uproarious laughter." "Enough", she roared. "Silence everybody, that's quite enough."

Johnny ruefully remembered, he got two hundred lines that day. "Think before you talk. Don't speak out of turn and stop day-dreaming."

Indira told him in the playground, that her uncle Ravi once hunted game in parties of ten or sometimes more elephants. Phandra, a renowned tracker knew every metre of the Shranghi estates, north of Delhi, near to where she had been brought up.

Indira's dark eyes, the whites like saucers, grew wider. "You know Johnny, there are eight tigers, some killers of humans, to each kilometre of over five hundred square kilometres. These tigers revile men, determined to maul and eat him. That is why they must be hunted to death."

His father laughed at him when he got home, late from school. But his mother was angry. "Don't laugh! Why, he's late home again! Now your food's got cold. I suppose you'll want me to reheat it for you!"

Stan winked at him across the room, from the table where he sat working.

"What are you doing dad?"

He replied, "I'm putting some of these old photo's away in this album. They're just some war-time pictures I found in the attic. I thought they'd been lost. You can see 'em, after you've eaten your steak and kidney pudding." He continued, "There are about a hundred snaps taken with my brownie. All in black and white film. That's all we had in those days."

Some were tinted in gouache or watercolor, with carefully laid thin green washes, delineating horizontal skies from landscapes.

"There ", said Stan, pointing to a batch of some twenty-five. "Taken in '39, '40, during the summer, before the fall of Singapore. I was in the R.A.F., Servicing hurricanes. You'll agree son, lots of smiling faces, friendly people. But I could never speak or interpret the native language. Somehow these yellow people all look alike, don't they!"

Stan and Johnny both laughed till the tears rolled down their cheeks. And the sounds of the crockery banging together grew louder and louder from the kitchen.

"How the camera wasn't confiscated when the Nips got us, beats me "said Stan. "Anyway, the rest of these are of our imprisonment in Burma." A lot of the shots were badly faded and yellow curled. "Small men, like dwarfs, mostly scowling there" said Johnny.

"They're the Imperial Japanese, our guards! Cruel blighters in wartime. Treat you like animals! If you tried to escape, you were shot, hunted down to extinction. The camp rats were the real survivors. They had it all cut-out! We had only six ounces of unpolished, half boiled rice rations per day. No wonder dog-eat-dog; we did! The rats and wild dogs ate many more of us than we had of them. Especially after the long marches….!"

Stan worked for the car manufacturers at Stockport, as a chief executive for quality control. He nearly resigned when there was a majority agreement to affiliation with the Japanese Corporation Suzuki.

"What! After that, a lot put us through during the war. Not bloody likely!"

Then he went abroad on invitation. Free flight tickets and five star hotel booking with the wife, to meet the Japanese contingent, Yuki Sumu, of Osso-Suziki Incorporation. They went initially for a whole month and sent air-mail letters home.

"Having a lovely time. Stan's met some really fine people! Quite a reunion in Okahama. The future looks good. Eating delicious food. Love from Stan and Sheila."

Enclosed in the packet was a small colour-photo included, of them both in kimonos, surrounded by errant geishas! On the back it said, "We've been given two miniature Pekinese. After quarantine, they can share your bedroom. They eat bamboo shoots, dried carp fish, with mushroom sauce. It is the custom here to bow to the rising sun."

They left twenty-five pounds behind for extras, to the well stocked larder and heaped freeze. Stan had satisfied himself that it was safe for his ten year old son to use the microwave. "He's bright Sheila. Why, any animal or monkey fool can manage.." Or, "What are you saying! We're insured aren't we? After all, it's all laid out!"

Having convinced himself that the little 'Wise-Muller' was able, Stan wrote out comprehensive recipes for the tastiest meals, together with heat settings and amounts of soap powder used daily in the dish-washer. Sheila said, "Don't forget to turn off the kettle switch!"

It wasn't just that Johnny was lazy. He was into visual excitement. His real problem was dyslexia. He feigned cleverness easily. Stan was too busy ever to read his school reports, while Sheila was either out working or rushing about cleaning the house, or playing bingo.

After four days away, Johnny got a telegram from Tokyo, the Hintlesham hotel at the airport was where they sent it. Johnny showed Miss Tatlin the letter. Miss Tatlin read out the title. "Please Miss, read the rest, I want to be sure!"

She glared cruelly at him, scrutinising his wretched, picked features and the drab grimy marks on his collar, including the wide seam below his greasy hair.

"It's an invitation boy, don't you see? They feel they must stay on longer, to honour the Emperor Hirohito and the Directors of the car company."

"I see, "said Johnny. "But how long is it for Miss, when will they be coming home?"

The vivid signs of apoplexy, like panting rhinoceros, bent upon immediate discharge, was startling in Miss Tatlin's features. "Idiot boy!" she said. "It states categorically that you must expect them home in another seven weeks time! That is, the twenty-first of September precisely! Write out, in clear lines, five hundred and fifty times, making no spelling mistakes, that 'teacher's time is precious!' And cease asking obvious questions and be less lazy!"

As a parting shot across his shivering timbers, she added, "Do these after school today. Tomorrow, I want to see you wearing clean clothes. You look like a ferret covered in mud!"

On the way home, Johnny noticed many mongrels parading and flirting amidst other puny members. Amongst puddles, the dogs tripped as though bemused looking into mirrors. Most had clean coats; the lean ones amused him, tail wagging towards the bigger fatter ones. Were these conciliatory gestures, fearful for their own strength and safety?

A little chocolate coloured terrier busily engaged in the licking of a large patched Dalmatian, ran forwards barking. He leapt up over Johnny's legs. The dog persisted and snatched his satchel away, making him run after this lively awkward animal.

It wasn't difficult to follow, what with the barking and the bumping of his leather bag along the pavement. Being a little fat, Johnny found the uphill run over Great Canal street and along, besides the Old Cotton Mill soon made him breathless. He eventually came to Nudger's Yard, a derelict site being converted into an amusement and leisure arcade.

Here the chase stopped before a vast wall. The dog he'd been after, sat panting at the far end of the lot. What caught Johnny's eye however was all the lurid paintings and graffiti, sprayed and splashed everywhere. Several strange young men in blue dungarees with unusual bobbed and coloured hair cuts were slapping on paint with full dripping brushes, amidst howls of derision.

Johnny ran down towards them. He wanted to read the squiggles and make out the funny wall pictures, as well as to catch and teach that cheeky dog a lesson. Suddenly, the whirling shapes of the paint and the leering faces snapped like brilliant neon lights inside his head. He was shocked to see that the boys had altered and were actually huge dogs, St Bernards, Pincers and Great Danes!

The colliding splotches clearly read out this startling message, 'Men for big dogs, are toys for small boys. We pick the fattest, lick their juiciest bones! We roam and scavenge! Run on, run to home! In packs we'll catch you, especially if you are alone!'

Johnny read this, pricking out all over in sweat. Turning, he fled as fast as legs could carry him! Never turning around, he got back home. The chocolate coloured terrier wagging his tail had followed. With battered satchel dragging behind, the terrier pressed the ledge with intrepid paws. The door swung open, welcoming him inside …

DOWN UNDER

Birt's mother got cold feet when she had him. Of her third sextet birth, Birt was the very last to arrive! What she saw then set her right back. Agnes stared at him much closer; he's such a very small Pip-squeak! She decided there and then she'd never again look close at anyone, especially her own Fred.

Dr Ryan prescribed hormone replacement therapy reluctantly, not to help her conceive. All he'd wanted was to get Agnes over her early onset of her menopause symptoms. Like her, Dr Ryan is a blackfella.

'Right from when Fred came to you, you Agnes was always so strong and swell, like a hearty basket. Round and always lovely! Fred's your partner is instead, a reed o' thin pale spinifex grass. This is you, keeping you strong and true!'

Dr Ryan continues, 'Here you are today, proud and raising your young uns. You've not changed much these ten years! 'Your skin; that's your concern?'

Agnes, 'Yes, my flushe's come and going..'

'Now you're dragging your feet ...' Let me see! Yes, you feel so tired! I'm sure bringing up these eighteen makes you tired at times! Yes! But you are still so young! 'He adds helpfully. 'Good. The hormone is good and helps. Gets a spring in your feet. You like it as it's the start of the year all over again.'

Agnes, 'Thank you.'

Dr Ryan is still shocked when Agnes recently had six more children. 'Why is the little one so white...you ask me? Is he a Whiteman's...No, no. I meant it is no freak of nature

..We Aborigines are Black as night ...'

Dr Ryan says 'Fred's a whiteman, as you and I, can't you see...? It's a real wonder to us both. All your children are black! That is the surprise we both recognise..That one, this last of your little sextet cluster... the very end of your latest batch. Birt is a blessing to your family...He can go anywhere in OZ land and be welcome..White is so OZ..Why are you so afraid of Agnes? You've given birth to one! He's such a gift..?!!!'

Agnes puckers her lip. Does not feel sure at all. Besides, Birt, her little boy barely stirs...As if he has not peered yet from out of her womb.

Fred, her partner, never looks-in that often anyways. 'I'm an I-TIE and finding peace work!!'

'A right good -egg' he calls himself. He meant of course he's no Italian! Fred is proud to be an itinerant Aboriginal; a free-loading work hand. He gives scarce attention to all the rest. 'My foundling baby!' Really, he's like this one. He takes such a greedy time holding and admiring Birt; are Fred's deepest expressions.

Agnes shudders and looks faraway. 'No good for man nor beast' she feels. Fred and Birt are not like the rest came from this OZ soil. One day the jigsaw fell together in Agnes's brain.

Fred always was restless, rootless and fancy free. She concurs 'His brains are fried and offers no help! Agnes blames the prolonged drought last summer.' She knows 'That's why he's tossed off one homestead to the next over again and again. Just gets in a few piddling days, and only rarely has a season's sheep shearing, at Goolagong, far away in Tasmania! '

Fred never earns or brings money home. He fetches driest salty mutton or only week-old lambs. They leap out of his hands the moment he returns home."No-good rearing' them!" Agnes says.

Fred smugly reminds her "Our sprogs adore witchetty grubs. I will find them tomorrow 'cos that's historical food."

Fred can't discern the shape or identity of Ostrich or kangaroo from crocodiles. Watching Fred scuttle off to hunt Ostriches; Agnes knows he's mistaken again!

Fred gasps, "Took me three days to find, but if you've nothing else for supper they are there! Poor weak lambs we'll eat them, half-weaners 'cos there's nowt else but Chitterlings. Ostrich's eggs ain't popular!"

Agnes covers her low Eucalyptus trees, collecting drops of moisture for her beds of Warrigal greens. Growing abundantly and tasting like spinach, they trail over the dry sandy gulches where little else lives. She attentively feeds her brood these greens, making them all strong. Birt and Fred won't touch it...Agnes says "That's why these two are so pale!"

Dr Ryan says "How well your children have grown."

She cannot tell him how proud she is with what they've achieved. Eleven years have passed. All fifteen they judiciously attend the new Christian Fellowship school two miles north.. "Its Birt, and Fred's fault! "Agnes tells the doctor, "They both bring out the worst in me, going for weeks into the bush alone!"

Agnes is angry. "I told Birt. 'He's my black sheep!"

She couldn't bring herself to say I told Birt, "You're a dwarf with a white face, like a witchetty grub!"

Fred says to them both: "Do you remember Jackaroo?" He's offering help. He says" 'Tell Birt, come to England to stay!"

Fred's chalking scripts on his grandfather's boomerang. He can neither read nor write.

Agnes then really knew there was news coming. "Watch Out! Fresh interest!"

Fred starts throwing his boomerang again. Something very different is going to happen!

Agnes recalls that time when Fred's half cousins came. Fred shows Agnes his cousin's faded photograph of this man, Fred's cousin with a familiar face, wearing a suit and glasses. Fred is there, wearing only a loincloth.

"Jackaroo. He's my cousin! "Fred points out: "Jackaroo got this weird skill, smelling oil fields, turning minerals into wealth!" Fred affirms, "He's very rich. Can you believe it! An OZ businessman! Educated and resourceful. Not like me!"

Agnes stares long and hard at Jackaroo's very neat suit and tie.

"Fred says he wants to meet you and me and right now he's living far away in England. We are going to Brisbane tomorrow."

Dr Ryan helped them out flying Agnes and Fred flew into Brisbane in the flying doctors plane. Jackaroo arrived carrying a big hamper he'd bought over, from a famous United Kingdom store named 'Fortnum and Masons. '

Under the stars outside of Brisbane where she and Fred first met in the heartland of the remotest bush that afternoon they all dined on Chicken and Champagne- the first for Agnes and Fred!

Jackaroo had been patient listening to Agnes, visiting Birt and all his other brothers and sisters.

It took a lot of persuading to even get him on board at first, but Birt finally got away. Jackaroo hired a car at Heathrow. Birt's pygmy size means he's just tall enough to take-in the strange surroundings. He's standing the whole plane journey on his toes. He gawps to take in everything out of the windows of the cars and planes.

Birt reveals to Jackaroo, "The world's flat..Mother says! She's a 'Flat-Earther. She insists ' Birt, you are a 'Good-For -Nothing Boy!! If you fly, you'll fall off the Earth's sides..' Mother wants me to be like all the rest, turning my hand to anything."

"Birt," she pleads, "EEk out a living!" Agnes says, "Birt, you're lazy like Fred, your father!"

She insists he's "Living-For-Free; Escaping, doing nothing every day in the desert!"

She often says to me, "Get Out'a Here..!!! You're delinquent like your father! Mother is wanting to have babies and needs me to go away!!"

Jackaroo is very happy how pleased Birt is, seeing everything. He's laughing and overjoyed at the bright London sights and sounds this first time.

"Uncle" Birt says, "I was getting so fed-up with deserts. Back there in OZ. This silent ghostly land.."

Birt's now soaking up driving in this spanking shiny car. He cannot believe the splendour of these grand houses passing and the greenness of the parks.. He's laughing!

"This is fun! The very best fun ever! Thanks for having me over! Flying's a WOW! Soaring higher and higher! Going up, then down under the clouds, out of the sky. Such a wonderful pleasure to me!"

They both stride into Jackaroos wife's kitchen, here in Frogmore Street, London SW18. Myra has all her fourteen children staying with them this Christmas! All turn around smiling and laughing between them, over the Big Turkey steaming hot on the middle of the table!

They all say, "Happy Christmas Birt and Jackaroo!"

Myra adds, "And you, my dear Birt! "she adds. "How great! You have come! You like tucker! I'm told you can't cook, so tuck in with us my little fella!"

Jackaroo said, "Yes, I learnt a long time ago, you don't have to do nothing! This holiday season's growing good. We're all being best at eating!"

LITANY OF BELLS

This is the incorrigible recollection from one object: part coloured cochineal, crushed juices from emerald river beetles, and these Incas, gatherers of water reeds, tying, knotting and weaving for llamas along the great Amazon river. Each Indian carries cherished, yet lowly votives: metal bells ornamenting to please, with offerings and music.

Workers - above ants, moving monumental stones: built through the jungle: Megaliths- gouged to beat and scourge, arresting dark tribal desires, electing the golden firmament.

Carry this: loads of ore, smelting, to separate base humours and so bring substance along. The long packs of llamas in lines, harnesses singing, carrying music and precious gold metals noting harvests; burgeons of Elderados for the Sun King, across Lake Titicaca.

Years pass: trials of war continue..

Another line, pack mules; orders and trappings, in feeding columns: Picks and shovels weighing, climb to the front for relief of the platoons.

Tom hears, like all private combatants, arterial fire- snagging metal, searing above, crescendos criss-crossing. The fiery star bursting air: piercing, deafening:

"I am numb- my body is bent, pin pricked: in submission to attritions."

Tom speaks: "Benumbing the pain, I listen to old reminders close to me- horse and mule dressed in clinking bits, horse brasses of this cavalry battalion, these 'bells' in my ear engross as I search for sluices, watery ways under duckboards.

Orchestrating rivulets take me: Shifting, marches. With organ brass band music administering."

Tom touches the harness ... "Ah..the horse: I mistook it!"

He reaches for the other animal, his mule: It's so dark, except for the shadows dancing to explosions: percussions go off, strobe and flutter-endless, bright and die; cascade, search and flood..Tom touches brocade. Feeling, not seeing enough- only the faint spiel outline of harness plain, like a toy. Simple yet familiar- enough for Tom to recount himself:

'Dancing': Thinking of his mother and sister in the church as she rings the bells..Then his mind's eyes recall..'Tere, that is how it is..his arms and legs down to his feet with bells..! Tressed like white lights. Silver and leather as they sound- step by feet falling, leading to chime each early year on this, that day out on this Village Green- England celebrating-May Days- Merrily ringing.

Solid chains of metal...The ground is shaking: Juddering loud and jolting. The sudden jar of crunching loads brings Tom back. He turns:

A bolt from over the ridge slues down, wedging his head into the exploding ground of falling shells:

Mud..Colluding, whips and rolls- up-vaulting: scattering all along the trench: Men, mules stagger- shiver, slide, cry out!

Green uniforms, legs, arms, leather and bridles: yet it is these 'rings and cups' separating, wrest and tear, beat out other tones, 'belling-points': and climbs: carrying the faint but tender insistent peal of bells:

Gradually as the battle thrall brings in Armistice- grasses return. The landscape breathes: Life returning, cultivating a clean atmosphere for refreshing earth, slowing..

One decade, then another goes..reaching for golden memories: "Stand near to the bright window..Look, the sun!!!"

Margaret is only ten. Her Aunty Hilda was a bell-ringer in the local parish, and her brother Tom. Margaret sees his photo before he got killed in Arras 1916, was a Morris Man.

"Aunt Hilda",Margaret notes: "This, these bells, with plaits on your mantelpiece - 'four bells' (she shakes them) See! With twinkling sounds!"

Aunty says: "Yes, they remind me of Tom. As I got older- I have arthritis now- I chime them, make a sound like church bells-only hushes one, are more quiet!"

"Where did you find them? Are they English?" Margaret asks."South American, maybe?"

Hilda laughs, "That's clever! I am told Limas or donkeys wear them, are decorations, worn around their heads..Tom's father had been there, that's where they are from!"

2221 arrives. Arras like all Europe is quiet, overgrown and wild. Bell-like Saucer ships emit a collection of sounds. So faint rising. It is pulsing. More than one in symmetry, synchronising. A signal certainly.

From the flannel grey sky a soapy opalescence bursts open and closes-like eyes:

Below charred, caving crumbling roofs. All around the robots are broken and still. The metal has changed, turning as the wind plays over the round balls, still falling out from the sky. Comets of javelin flowers, are opening by the sun.

Each bell chimes, rippling out delicate, solarised, electric. Building together: an orchestra of harmonising music, running up from the Amazon river to the Danube.

WINTER'S TALE

Thomas said, "The long icicles upon the house gutters are like walruses sabre-teeth, or polished swords."

Always quick to parry, his sister Gemma remarked, "They're big stalactites or Merlin's finger nails, glass like and sharp as daggers."

The gusting north-west wind was spiralling down the chimney, while outside, the creeping smoke fell across the white lawn and the snowy fields. Billowing like long fishing nets, it was slowly moving metre upon metre, majestically into the white coloured distances.

The black ice slide was a shining, dark brittle treacle near the driveway. For the second time during any tumbles, Michael awkwardly sat at the edge of the run, considering his curious glazed reflection. His natural, pink complexion showed up pinched across his nose and ears, while his sparkling teeth looked icy cold and he started to chatter. Just then, a snow-thing whizzed past his right ear, and dipping down, penetrated the snow surface of the ground.

"Watch-out!" he shouted and quickly scrambled upon his feet, reaching to grab-up immediately with his icy hands, a hard packed pile of snow. As he did so, out of the corner of his eye, he saw Phillip's form ducking down sneakily behind the garden shed. Perhaps anticipating a chase , he sped off towards the shelter of a nearby orchard, across the lawn. Like two hounds, they tore past the snow laden garden pond and bushes, and the remainder of chewed dog bones, scattered and half-buried.

Two blue tits and a robin were taking turns to tunnel holes into the creamy marrow. All along the fence beside them, black birds, field fares and thrushes were foraging beneath the ice-crusted leaves, making meals of wind- fallen apples.

Tom and Gemma had built the snowman before she gathered coal bits, then buttons from her mother Mary's sewing basket, choosing a fresh looking carrot from the vegetable bin in the kitchen. "Come on Thomas" she implored, "I'm ready with the items." She lugged at the loose tartan wrapped about Toms' neck, as he sat snug, drying beside the fire. Finding little success, she then sped off with his slippers, up and down the stairs until he agreed to come outside again.

They set off past the drive where Peter, their father, was still working, shovelling away the overnight snow-drifts, piling them up like dirty lump-salt on either side, along the lawn. "Take the dog, won't you?" was all he said and Thomas hastily fetched Hew, the eager terrier.

Halfway down the old byway track leading towards Copples farm, Tom stood motionless, unnoticed by Gemma who continued ambling along; throwing sticks with encouraging orders to Hew, who chased and sometimes retrieved them. Across the valley, away in the distance below, were two specks outlined against the boundary side of the field, before the snow blasted, black forest.

The winter cabbages here were fodder for many creatures. Tom saw partridge and pheasants and once, the rare fleet form of a fox, dancing in the dappled light of Autumns' turning foliage. He remembered how it came on, running in and out of the broken barley stalks. He wondered if it was playing a game! Then, appearing ahead, darting like an exocet missile was a chased rabbit, fleeing terrified from the pursuers clutches. Then suddenly, it flung itself back from where it had emerged, into the enclosing trees.

Now Tom was watching two other animals, common roe-deer, a buck and doe! They cautiously took turns to stand sentry and graze; holding their heads erect, straining for menacing scents or threatening sounds. Like exquisite rare visitors, vulnerable in targeted positions, one perceived danger was always enough to send them recoiling and bounding away; their white down-turning tails into cover. Yes, already they were gone! Tom wondered if they had heard the excited growling barks of Hew, rising like amok gunfire.

The crump of dry compacted snow beneath his footsteps soon resumed, accompanied with the snorting, snuffling noises from Hew by his side. Then ahead, among the track below where Tom guessed was the likely position of Gemma, there flew up from amidst the hazy-shrouded trees, a tumult of startled pheasants and pigeons. In an instant, there followed the delayed thundering report of a shot-gun, punching the silences, rolling loudly and echoing through the iron-cold air.

Hew, evidently frightened, gravely barked back, while Tom stood in his tracks, awaiting further shots to go off. Finally he said, "Hew", (who meanwhile had chosen to plunge and career about in the deepest pockets of snow) "come on boy, let's catch up with Gemma." But like all obstinate Scottish terriers, he chose to obey in his own time, following after, only about a hundred feet or so.

As the track widened, coming level at the bottom of the valley, it started to snow. Like fine dusty sleet at first, soon the flakes came on heavier., Until Toms' coat and face was besieged by the down pouring blizzard. All he could see of Hew was a small tousled thing, flopping about the fast disappearing path. So short had the distance ahead become to his vision, that he scarcely knew which way to turn. "Gemma!" he called out, "Where are you?"

Then he realised that it was probably impossible both to be heard in this maelstrom or to expect either to catch sight of her just yet. Near to them, he remembered there were some old, very tall holly bushes to shelter beneath, until the snow storm had subsided. For in this prevailing mess, it was quite useless to expect them to continue their walk.

He imagined Gemma ending up over the snowman, adding the carrot-nose and then the coal-buttons to his chest, pressing the worn pipe of their Grand-pa's into his mouth. "I hope she doesn't add my scarf too "and laughed. It seemed ironic in the gloom. The snow man was nearly ready, paunchy and round upon the top of the hill, overlooking their village. Only yesterday, he had finally made it, just before dusk. There hadn't been time to quite finish him off.

Gemma grew fuming but silent in a strange, purposeful anger. Finally she said, "Okay, clever clogs, let's see! We'll build him again, much bigger this time around." They had worked together, hardly stopping from lunchtime until it grew dusk. The snow figure had eventually been completed, taller than they had dared to expect. He was all of four feet in girth and a massive, nearly six foot high!

Tom stood shattered beneath the holly, deep in thought, when Hew came spontaneously alive, barking for all his mite into the thick falling snow. "Stop you silly beast!" Tom prevailed, "It's only Gemma, finding her way back." Sure enough, out of the swirling cold flurries, there came hurrying along a figure. It appeared to be staggering as though blinded, awkward because of the severe conditions.

Tom strained his eyes, barely able to see his own hand, let alone Hew or his sister. Hardly had he brushed the congealing snow out of his own eyes, when the person, or whatever it was, plunged on past, knocking Tom into the hedge! At the same time, the figure trod right upon his dog and Hew squealed in abject terror.

Tom rapidly picked himself out of the deep bank of snow and soothed the frightened terrier, whose tail wagged yet whimpering beside him. "Never, ever have I seen anything like this before in my life." Tom, like Hew was shivering; "I don't believe this" he said, shaking his head. "It's incredible! It was as if our snow-man came alive, walking down from the hill, stirred awake by his fresh snow!!!"

They both stood, then sat down, rooted and numb as the wind tossed snow grew lighter and fell away gradually to nothing. Then they got up and stumbled off down the path to resume their search for Gemma. They found her, less than a hundred metres away, sheltering under a yew tree.

She was crying and was very relieved to see them. Her first words were, "The snow-man, did you see him? He was here and he snatched out of my hands the bag containing those things we had come with for him!"

Her sore eyes looked frightened and pained. "I mean" she continued, "He rushed by on this path, past me and I heard him saying it was too cold on that hill!"

Gemma started to laugh. "His voice was gruff you know, like grating broken glass!" She mimicked him, "Give me my coat buttons and the carrot nose! With the coals, I have need eyes to see!" Gemma went on, "Then he disappeared up along the path, like the abominable snowman." Tom nodded, "Yes I saw him! Poor Hew too!"

Tom and Gemma and Hew walked on until they came to the site where only yesterday they had built and left their snowman. Sure enough, hard as it was to believe, he was gone. Only a small hollow remained where the heavy giant had stood. Tom started to speak, but Gemma just laughed. "Come on "she shouted, "Let's have a snow fight, before it all melts away!"

A short distance beyond the brow of the hill, Tom came across a man in the possession of a gun, who also had bagged several birds, probably pheasants from that recent shooting. Gemma said, "We heard you shooting from back-up the path."

The small bald headed man replied, "I'm pleased to see you. I'm out for my usual Saturday shot. I hardly expected to see much, certainly no game you see. I had just come into this clearing, and well…I did see something!!!"He had become quite pale and the pipe in his mouth shook and jumped about in his mouth.

Exasperation gripped Gemma; she grabbed his arm. Both she and Tom blurted out together, "What was it, please tell us. What did you see?" Cedric's eyes bulged and both his pipe and his hat nearly fell from him. "I still can't believe it, the biggest snowman I ever saw, like a ten ton white tennis ball! And it shot down this same hill, flying along this path!"

He continued, "I had been sighting my gun ready for firing, before the storm you appreciate, upon a nearby hazel grove, at some pigeons. I looked up, suddenly aware that snowing had started, when I spotted the snowman figure swaying, yes swaying up there!"

He had pointed his gun again towards the hilltop. "I naturally thought at first the snow had blurred my vision. Then before I could stir myself, the snowman, for that's surely what he was, had come alive! In a twinkling of an eye he was off, falling fast as you could caper, towards me! The snow came on exactly at that moment. My gun went off and this beast went by me, grating his teeth and saying, 'Away with you: snow is free!' That was all!"

Cedric looked aghast. "He went up that path there." He pointed to where they had just come from. Tom said "I know, we saw him too!" Cedric nodded, "How strange, how awfully odd indeed!"

BLACK SPIDERMAN

Rico was stripped then hurled down into his cell. He began a count. One smear, then more..Soon, counting no longer figures as days turn into years. Shit in the precise same place to keep time and a record.

The guard Grava barked."You stay back. Go against the far wall."

Through the tiny observation slot he threw his food onto the floor, splattering over Rico's feet. Again Rico's anger exploded in him, powerful to kill..He knows if beaten, retaliate. Yet any moves to make way or alter his crushed lot by direct defiance for now is beyond him.

Thrown to wolves he's abject. Rico beats the walls until his fists bleed. Brainwaves had shifted towards stupor or delirium without stimulation. Bleeding lips knotted his dried out tongue. The black punch-bag of his body sways and has sagged. Rico's aching heart and shattered brain is a vilifying barracking rhythm.

In Rico's previous stay in Santa Monica's open prison, he was ecstatic to have books, spending days reading the same paragraph over and over again, not being able to understand anything and just hurling it at the wall in frustration. Before, there were notes, I mean writing we shared.

"Prisoners then survive. Learn as natives."

Prisoner number 3469, or Mr Mooth told Rico, 'I am a Crow Indian. I killed a white oil prospector.. Destroyed my family when they took away our homestead, laying a pipeline. We Indians lost indigenous folkways long ago. Defiance is the savage way! Do that! Be cunning! Act with no action. Overcome adversaries; learn stealth."

Against rules, all prisoners find ways to make human contact. Find ways around the world. After all, punishment will not be swift; instead of an executioner's hand these rebels will be left to rot.

'Kite-flying' is a game children play; another form was folding over and over as a line of a poem or a secret code to break was written on paper to give away a suggestion, providing an answer to a problem, sharing a plan waiting to hatch. Prisoner's got around authority and crushing confinement by clandestinely passing notes.

Look. The words came imploring in the dark of the night. 'Crane for waking! See inklings arising up before you. Stare for each second and find a wisp of leaf, a tiny tear of paper.'

Rico stealthily kneads along the cold concrete floor, feeling the edge of the door. He reaches for news, pitiless in his torment for each thread slipping, posting. Live eels swim up before him, wriggling in dry desert gulches to bring signs of life. In this long blinding firmament are melting spaces, out there, beyond manacling walls. Voices or stars turn, promising flashes bring visions and freedoms. These are a lifeline when you are broken, lost in overwhelming despair.

Letters stuck, pieced into words one by one. 'Razor-blade.' Another week passed. Then soft threads came daily: spelling T, O, W, E, L. The guard Grava was careless. Rico discovered along the top edge was concealed a razor-blade fragment.

Pain pitches Rico to act. His total deprivation forces him to desperation. He splits Jailer Grava's jugular. With keys and guns Rico's force breaks down all bars. He goes outside, flees away. He looks but is forgone, blind and bereft. Facing no resolution, he is purged and is captured quickly. Rico is sprung by anger he could not contain. Obstructed at every level, he is denied by each stage and a person who has everything when he has nothing. To make a new life in the open path he was in beyond prison, finds him with no hope of any redemption.

Back inside after killing again by anger and desperation, Rico's gut-wrenched isolation falls into a huge well. Black hopelessness becomes egregiously more deep and dark. In silence hell bound noises creep up to him.

Always recalling. Rico remembers 'I haven't seen a tree or plant since 2003, neither have I met or spoken to my father since 2000. The only thing that I saw is a black spider waiting to beat me soon to pulp in the corner.'

Rico finds little bugs sometimes. "Are they cockroaches? I save up these moments like I got a pile of riches or gold when I have nothing but this rat."

He tries to keep awake, to deny it a chance to bite him. He is petrified, as he anticipates it is waiting to eat him. Rico then feels it gnawing at his putrid guts inside.

"I am in torment, of this my suicide, waiting to take over, each twenty-two hours in this cell."

One night he woke shivering in the cold cell. Only a faint light shone over his face and naked torso. He sat up in terror! Radiating beads are marching towards his mouth. He could see their mandibles, all red driving and cutting into his skin. Up to his chin, his chest was covered in innumerable shiny weevil insects, radiating beads marching towards his mouth.

Rico stealthily kneads, feeling the edge of the door, patient for each thread slipping, posting to him. These are codes and signs of life in a long blinding firmament. Here they become voices or stars turning like a flash, as a dream towards visions and freedom windows. These actions are a lifeline when you are almost mentally and physically broken, lost in overwhelming despair.

One night thinking 'this is my thirtieth' he felt something alight upon his nose, light like a feather. To him so close, he saw piercing eyes staring intently. These were what he had just dreamt. The creature moved its legs incessantly and as it opened its jaws, it let out a shrieking tirade of fire.

This conversation between himself and a spider continues. Fire pours into a stream that is acid, devouring his last hopes. The dream drives away the dark, heralds the roof. Rico is no longer in his cell. The wind and the sky is dark, he has got outside! His sight takes in the roof, turning Rico inside out.

"I am here on the top of the prison."

He looks down at the yard and steadies his sinews. A tingling shiver courses up and down his thin wiry filamented legs. Stretching up, he lunges into attack! His blue gorging tongue hauls in the fly as his legs spring; his mouth trap open, mashing it down.

The black spider swiftly casts a line. Holding on securely, he crosses over the roof. Rico, aware of his new defying freedom realises the spider has also snared a trap for him.

"Where are we? What do you want from me?"

Rico is frightened, yet also so thrilled to be another shape, one with this insect!

The black spider says, "All you have is what I want, to be so near and able to dominate a human being! You are going to die very soon. You want revenge, to kill all those who have been so merciless, right!? Well now watch! First we cut the electricity."

Stepping down, the black spider slides deftly inch by inch outside of the prison walls. As it moves it clasps Rico tightly and continues its shrieking tirade.

"First I'll suck the life from the Prison Governor.. The prisoners shall flee and be caught in my web. After that's done you'll die, absorbing your life's juices to become a spider!..."

REAL KEEPER WALKING

Over the horizon the pointing fire lifts with the red opening star. The sun's ray sends the first light spear casting a rose light; two hooks rise open, go clear: The under chassis of the figure bathed in light glances newly upon lumpy knees, their clay-like cracked shields quaking with the bathing light awakening: dancing from the rising trunk swinging and dapples across the elephant's tail as it bounds rolling,, going forwards.

Out from liquorice black night a sandwich finger of two colours step. One foot after the other thrusts and lands in light gestures. Ably walking so quietly, the foot rocks onto toes that are the last thing to leave the ground. White nails fall behind mat-brown shadows of each flesh planter.

The rear foot is placed onto the same spot just vacated by the front foot. The shifting feet lift under its own tremors, go folding forwards, thrusting stealthily in force. Mounting steadily, it's mobilising movement rises loping and slewing, sloping forwards and down - treading in remorseless motion as road dust also rises.

The way is hushed, so early before anyone else, before morning. There are no other signs of life, nor any vehicles yet passing along the road. As the bare nails bear heavy stomping and lump, it's driving feet one by one press and flow, beating in a dancing rhythm. In slow tread of time it's edgy trotting moves easing, the pace of the feet drives. Moving forward the determining feet carry jostle and quickening motion, hastening more… Easing forwards, stomping with an easier life motion in this strange new land.

Where is this traveller from? Inside he wrestles with old pains to overcome:

"Tolerance, resignation..such misery pressed into, to conform to a world that was not my own. If one of my kind falls ill or dies, Europeans simply bring another of my kind from my old homeland. In dark past shadows ghosts of these refugees are lingering. Their legacy lives on; scattered throughout the world are thousands of elephants, all dependent on human care or lack and woeful misunderstanding. Each of us, individuals, of belonging, separated from our ancestral herds has a story to tell, with the past, a present and hopefully a future."

Emerging in dawn's opening curtain, shadows lighten and turn glinting. In colliding grey wings, particles of dust climb. A squalling tide falls behind. Propelled between hedges and the bare earth, pink edges the feet.

Out ahead, the feet follow with insistent steppings, determined - drawing upon its own purposes. Bestowing creases to ankle shapes as light eddies upwards. The shade of the flesh tinted, freshened as the landscape slips and slinks marking the passing passageways. The treading figure segues past subways and houses. Unveiling higher almost to the knees, the feet rise straining emboldened, refocusing as light silvers over the blurring suburban streets.

The thick hewn feet upon solid legs move readier by each stride, sensing country air and natural tree landscapes unfolding. The breaths are deep like the currents of his driving limbs turning into active delivery. Deep swishing sounds of walking in active devotion besides wayside grasses motioning through his ears, merging with his own breaths, recoiling and returning…

Out shoots, a growling deep trumpeting voice:

"I broke out: I could not be contained. I stood on the metal links. The fence I tore away.!! Keepers said they wanted to keep us all moving so they used bull hook's aggressively. Some of us already were pitiful and weak, slowed by arthritis and terrible foot rot. My cousin was actually euthanized because of her foot problems. social isolation or lack of complexity in the physical environment. Many suffer nail cracks and abscesses on our soles. Keepers though brutal have no knowing as we do and elephant's foot-related problems lead to euthanasia for captive elephants. I had to get free…That kind of behavior is cruelly so misguided… There were puncture wounds on both her trunk and her feet, her shoulders, head, back, hip and ears …If they had only let her go, like me…"

He lifts again, calling louder, blows clear and high. Motions mount yet as oceans carry and give over to him faint calls. He steals, feels sensing faraway, tintinnabulations, of beryls and peal's. Loadstone of instincts, first memories and insistent freedom, stir urging him still. Crossing from enclosure to the one direction, clambering into the freeway faraway continent of wild Africa…He is moving, A tread of separation from the pain of loss, from Spain.

"I am an elephant and I escaped from that place my keeper calls a zoo, it is a circus of pain. I like all my kind have tremendous space requirements because of our massive size and being. We are also highly social and very powerful, built to cover and roam a large amount of territory, building healthy muscles and healthy strong feet. Only then can we enjoy a good strong skeleton experiencing differing climates and terrains."

His mother answers her son's stress and lonely loss so far away from her life. "Wild elephants walk up to 100 miles a day. Able to move through forests and large savannas and we were actually from a desert in Mozambique, moving on sand, a desert as well, so they had a variety of ways in which to move and are very active and we're able to cope supremely well."

He replies, "In the confinement we endured, in this Zoo or circus the restrictions took a severe toll. Our energy is almost entirely pent-up in these small spaces, causing natural behaviours to be blocked and bad things thrive mentally and physically, producing dual lasting damages to us."

The holding call is journeying to a bridge and a causeway, crossing from Spain into Morocco, way beyond.. far away, towards Africa and where there are forebears, his own waiting…

The great trunk of the young elephant noses up, sensing the smell of ozone, of salts. Into the arch bracts of his wide dish -like ears he hears distinctly far off calls, bringing to the inmost soul other voices, lighting up the returning returning sounds, of a familiar moving herd…Certain also is the rumble sent to toll, brings like a chord of triumph, his mother arches, re stepping nearer to his own hemisphere. A thousand long journeys of one more thousand kilometres transecting each of them. He heard the voice come to her. Her son, she also has figured, is returning.

WOLF PACK

Colonel Strike led the Wolf-Pack of scouts up Kilder Pass in Derby. They marched in formation. This is a seven day trip. Edward and his friends had started the summer holidays, waving goodbyes to parents. Spree-time, camping in the hostel grounds. "We're going down Kilder Dyke, sometimes trekking and camping, then into Blue John's. Whatever that is?"

At the camp the wind's rose, getting under the bivouacs. An old man spoke about the hill climb. "Keep on the track, watch-out for sudden descents and mists. Them will o' wisp snares and Hags and magicians: these are traps and spells, hidden warnings beware!"

Out of the blue, Colonel Strike became ill. The message relayed is "Keep to your posts. The second in command Marshall Beam does not come. What orders?"

Mysterious bumps occurred that evening. Everyone gets confused: excitements and strange rumours beat about cross-wires from lights sighted from the hills with mysterious singing surges. Then, flying low above the camp a drone and enlarging, as a plane arrives. Parachutes and hampers descend. Open messages on furling ropes drop straight in. The message says: "Put on the costumes. Let us all play!"

The games started; children ran amok, dressed as clowns. Acting like giddy-aunts shouting: "Who let off the smoke bombs?" Everyone wore masks as the boxes opened. It starts with playing first 'blind man's buff', then 'cops and robbers. Camp leader Fox shouts out a game-order: 'Bonkers at broncos, rider's jump onto wild horses!'

Everyone formed lines and danced in a great circle: No one knew, because of the costumes, who-was- who! Edward's head was filled by drowning-out choruses and big noisy shouting. As he strained to see and hear from between the trees, lots of playing chimps emerged. Three camels sidled in, then one bison, a lion with ten cubs and lots of cows.

Held in by the awe of the crowd, Edward saw and was moved by the throngs. It was like in the cinema, feeling the thrill as you sit back and grow smaller. As marmosets, with eyes enlarged, watched-out, a pantomime of dramas opened. Disguises altered, grew privy to a stranger's captivation! Breaking upon the little people, the forces of a stranger life, gremlins gathered, grew in size and numbers.

Wizened boggarts, others with yellow skin, brushed past. Cackling green-eyed witches prodded the wolf-scouts. They pressed, playing with horns and pawed tauntingly anyone in a bright costume. One wizard held two white rabbits in each hand. Then they flew up, clapping their wings furiously and turning into fantail pigeons!

A bus drew up, followed by three more on the hill. The first conductor shouts, "Everyone! Attention please! Get on board!" He has a blue face and red eyes. On the second and third bus are as many as a hundred animals. All are playing kazoo, tambourines and castanets. As Edward clambers on getting a seat, the bell rings. The engine thunders into life, chugs off and gathers great speed. Hurling off down the hill at breakneck speed, Edward clings on, peering back at the tents pitched still on the hill side.

A star bursts above them as the bus draws up into a wooded clearing. The conductor and driver steps down and confirms, "Get down here, we have arrived at our destination! Scouts with tickets must stay seated. Those without tickets must get off. You will be escorted to the castle."

Edward flushed. He has no ticket! He got up, stumbling off the bus. The conductor shouted again behind him, "You who remain are to encircle the castle. You must rescue these captives and succeed by morning, or the castle and everyone inside will be destroyed - burnt to the ground!"

A black hooded henchman-slayer met Edward and the Wolf Pack, all dressed up as harlequins, foot-light troubadours, unicorns and filibusters. Bezerk said, "This is my castle! With my wet-stone, fie and fum, I keep my axe blade super-scream sharp!"

The axe he swayed side to side, keeping time - swishing forwards, then back. It swayed in time with the castle clock's pendulums. Pointing upwards, Bezerk shouted: "If your help does not break in and free you all by tomorrow morning you're doomed to die! One by one, I'll cut-off your heads! I feed you each to my wolfhounds and pigs!"

The sun rose at five the following morning. The crowd and all the animals drew near to the lake. On a mount in the middle stood the black castle, all fortified and high turreted.

The old wizened one with a blue face, blue hands and a tall pointed starry hat spoke. "Last night we went on a journey and entered a cavern. From this hollow, strong we returned, bringing precious crystals. Soon now we are to turn the menace of Bezerk to our success and victory!"

The wizard bowed. "Ezra the Bold, I am. That's my name. Hold up your crystals 'til the sunlight shimmers upon them: See!"

All the crowd held up the blue-stone crystals above them. The sun light shone and broke out above them, breaking with fire, linking each one by one: Then fire shot forwards and ran like a volcano funnel. It shot on the water, streaming to the foundations of the castle. As the light burst stronger, it set fast making steps like a ladder and pathway across the water!

"Let us step across!" shouted Ezra: "We must storm the castle and defeat Bezerk! Take the castle and free our friends!"

As the crowd stormed the castle, up, up away rose the castle into the air! Bezerk's axe rose and fell, sweeping around in full circle, and cut off Bezerk's own head. The portcullis of the keep opened, as the clock swung backwards, catching the castle alight!

The castle instantly, like a falling balloon, swept over the lake, then dropped down over the campsite. The revellers returned to the ground as the ladder let go of its grapple irons. Everyone hung on tightly as they descended. No one removed their costumes - they just stood with blackened faces laughing!

A shriek went up! Black dressed menacing figures surrounded them. "We order you to lie down!"

They carried whistles, blowing them with piercing shrillness. Edward recognized the smoking canisters and automatic rifles - 'yes', he pondered, 'They're Gangsters, it's a heist!'

Suddenly, other roaring noises intervened. Blue lights and surging 'copter-blades ' blazed over them. A whirling of fanning beats came above them, then surged directly down, closing over them. Three helicopter's descended besides the emerging balloon. Marshall 'B' had arrived!

He called out with a megaphone over the crowd: "Pack up your tents boys, follow my trail. It's Wells Fargo! From now on it ' s follow me! As wolves, you have me as your leader, so only follow and take my order's alone! I'm Marshall 'B'! Let's go find some Indians on the trail!"

The Wolf-Pack jumped to their feet, ran forwards. Alighting hastily into the helicopters, up shot the 'copter's blades, rotating fast and then swiftly rising furiously. The Wolf Pack disappeared, spear-headed straight up into the clouds.

KNODELS

Across bare soil old bomb rubble strews. Every day. surrounding vast grey fields merge into cold damp mist. Using pick and shovel or bare hands, they halt, pounding stone boulders to dust.

It is early. Lines of men, hasten and trudge; carting busy lifting then moving rubble. All are wearing striped sack clothing. Using pick and shovel or bare hands, they halt, pounding stone boulders to dust. Shattering integuments, into emptiness. Vestiges of memories.

Gustave has worked here since his capture.

'Six months..My…'

Up at 4am. Dazzled by the summertime heat and grinding dross Gustave worked here late 1941:

'Rous Rous!!! '

The guards merciless with beatings: Gustave again recalls November tenth,.Kristallnacht

Bricks, rocks off the street, broke windows. I remember Franz, my father. Palpable shudders in everyone. How his hands lifted to protect my face..Rabbi Warbinger appeals. Halfway through his sermon.. 'My people..!!' The door bursts open suddenly and SR Brown shirts fall on us, shepherding us into the street. The guards are merciless with beatings: Broken glass fills the roads, under our feet…As we. numberless captives. defiled, start attention, roll-calls at Bergen-Belsen. Franz and mother have both disappeared.

Though wilting, the leaves feel almost cool around his feet. Potatoes need banking and moisture emerging from dust.

Gustave recalls before: ' How we worked!!! Truly satisfying. My father Franz loves clearing those common choking weeds like deadly nightshade and fat hen. '

'We stop now and eat this dish? ' That word's funny. ' Strudels! '

'No, it's 'Knodels! ' Franz says firmly: ' Here in the Rhineland. You get it. Yes!? Dumplings..'

'Of course! ' Gustave nods.

With juicy butter. Thoroughly well cooked. How right, drained well and so floury. It's their first dish together. A glowing recollection after suffering with Yamah..Mother had been so ill..Last fall Franz, with so many responsibilities..keeps all work going.

Landsmen here are supremely loyal..His labourers tireless, dedicated..Get well provided in return…

Franz had hoped for him. He's proud for his son, finally graduating as a metal worker. Gustav studies hard, gains real skills.

'Franz, father..'

You know I'm a fledged GoldSmith…Gustave firmly corrects him..' I practise, started this month in Leipzig..I hope you'll visit! '

'Yes…! Franz smiles wanly..'Of course..We must keep working..Nothing shall keep us. No upheavals or dreadful rumours! Our determination is to bring good harvests of potatoes!!. I grow Golden varieties. And you Gustave make prized vessels! I'm so proud of all you achieve..! '

'Move! March! '

Zonner-Commando Valf, appointed to execute all duties, points his rifle muzzle at Gustave. "Faster, Faster!"

He barks. In the distance is the Bowser. The thin, corpse-like group muster. They gather at one end of the huge metal carriage, press together to move and salvage the fading crop…Slowly, inching the dead casing, at last it slowly shifts..Heavy train wheels go sliding into sand, moving forwards..All day it takes to travel forwards, going imperceptibly towards the open trickle of water..The only irrigation that is..This moisture is the sewage from the inmates is so small..is already melting by the suns furnace heat …

Valf never stops beating and screams out "Take these!"

"Fill the Bowser," he screams..Handing out soup ladles..' Move now!"

As finally droplets gather, the crop of potatoes are fed..Daily the men shower sprinkles over the wilting leaves.

Gustave fetches, joins the thin weary men, driven to begin the journey yet again. Their shoulders heave and stab, gradually managing and pulling the huge bowser to the slow water course. The faint yellow stains still trickle, leeches into grey sands.

Before the night arrives Gustave delivers the last moisture and instantly melts into the dull potato leaves..

He's staring down, eyeing closely and reaching down. Frankfurt with surgeons steady hands..A golden thing, so round there..Meeting passions, black antennae perches towards him.

Opening his fist. His captive brindles with a bright orange carapace.:

Gustave recognises ' Leptinotarsa Decemlineata..I know you, Colorado Beetle.. Black-White..His clothing, They are similar; ten striped..This Ten-Striped Spearman.

He lifts his head, surveying the guards. For them potatoes provide salvation, bringing hope and a way out from starvation.

"What now?"

The Beetle sits on the potato, nestled, hidden in his hand..

Gustave answers, "Of course, famine follows pestilence.."

Like him, the beetle is dressed, 'one hydro yuk and one bith yuk in the middle. to its ankles. Each, with sleeves above elbows - as all the other inmates are clothed.

His fingers meet something on the ground, obtruding and attached in the roots. Gustav's dry lips utter silently:

"It is a sign.."

The potato looks so much like a golden ball. But it actually also smells of flesh. Precious and yet earthy, with moisture for his desperate parched lips. Gustave's hand reaches to his mouth, touching this round small golden potato Valf smiles. Pulls his finger, triggers..and aims.."These are the insects destroying our resources.."

Krrrrkkkkkkkkkkkk!

Gustave falls, hit between his eyes. The potato falls. The insect passes straight down into the soil.

"Gott!"

Valf drops his rifle down, then reflects:

"The air temperature is rising. Conditions are getting far too dry. Another body raises saturation, to help sustain moisture, Ja! One less mouth to feed.. It's good..Our common purpose truly sustains our potato crop. This heep is merely a dumpling - how apposite! Ein heep, Knodel."

THE BIER

In the bier, a glistening white flower peers at the sun.
And peace, more peace to Saint Francis.
The body cloth-wrapped, is ash; listen: the larks sing above.
Oiled and bandaged, with candles lit, his body rests upon rock.
Locked in shining embrace, the maiden Moon looks on, at night
And the shaded mourners keep solemn wake in grey and white light.
Wreathed with the oils of junipers, the air is funerale;
The white roses are scattering petals upon the lawns of death.

The apple tree in the garden germinates, burgeons from the pip,
Out, forwards from desire realising darkness, spearing the turf.
The brown spear thickens and towers, turning a spindle of fern;
Green fingers, with green laughing leafy tears and red jewels,
Dropping sweetly to the soft and wet brown soil.

The eyes of the dead are hazed over, screened in tree blossom;
In Elysian flowering, it rends apart the curtains of the dead.
The impatient oxen, hoofs at the straw; Snakes hook under troughs,
slipping shining through the water.
Nightly, owls and frogs loosen fall, hoots and croaks.
A laughing bright child makes mud pies in the rain.

In Summer, flowers are eloping with athletic equatorial runners.
Each bears his fire-bearing torch, bone-shaking, with cheetahs Kangaroos
Mountain bounding, to the hot God, gift bringer.

What hoofs, wings, skin, thoughts, manes, and visions bring to him!
Arrows shoot, arms and stairs enfold the unending birth.
The sun comes to the breathing, opening and flowering creatures,
Art and work, the Olympian sun shines and sun life grows.
The Olympian sun makes the Olympian ceremony and Hymn.
In wine and wedding, Man and Women sporting in ceremony, courting.
The ether fishes are swimming, and bees of honey, humming!

Trumpeters and sweeping Angels are flying over white daisies,
Swaying the praying mantis, an energetic spirit on the wing.
The skulls look on, as festooning diseases of wars deepen.
The river Styx is bearing the victims and heathens to Hell.
Ravens on banners enact cruel parts at the head of black arts;
Here men shriek in their rage, sinking in sin, increasing age
As the choking earth is plugging up their shuddering open jowls.

The opals enamour the belly dancer of the seven veils.
Enchantresses with beguiling eyes catch beaus of their choice,
As white throated fish hang on hooked shrimps

And Salome' is carried upon the helm of a ship,
above gilded fauns, and unicorns,
foretelling the New Millennium
With the martyr and hind, golden fleece-bearing,
Out of the dark ancient woods, of the forlorn, aged storm.

The lotuses on the water are floating so white and flowering.
In the oyster cup, pearls, the goldfish, satin cheetahs',
Blue budgerigars', kingfishers, and rainbows with lupines.
Like Pharaohs sarcophagus, all more lasting.

The forever future of fading memories and the blowing winds of God.
The gusts of wind girding the courts and feathers of birds.

Cultures and the cloaks of Man see the waters slowly fall,
Going gushing down below, the invisible rushing clear,
As white waterfalls into the oceans, glad with splashing motion.
The creatures of God are in locomotion.
Their roots are placed within His station.
The glowing of our souls, beckon to His call,
As shadows lighten, awakening gallantly to His glad making day!

MATTA YOUR SOUL?

The crowd swelled behind and ahead, packing in, closing together. Sullenly not moving..

Someone reminds 'Our capital street Regent..Once held rumours, or false news. There were history books.. Real history recalled events..that happened.'

'Who? Sorry..Go on..'

Before mid 2050, an Apple store stood here. Vendors selling bananas..The Banana Republic..And when there were those computers..Microsoft run by a Billy..er..Gates. His spies from the other North end, Broadcasting House…announcing, unflinching: 'No more soup runs..The era of Austerity ends, No gentle reminder of what's missing..There is to be 'a Feast..!!!'

'Who said.? '.

Any mention sends people running..

Where? Sirens….Fires, warnings..only in civil shakedowns do the many go restless, hither..bother…Some go. Then want to return. Some plea-bargain for order. Deafness is benign..Crowds are crowd minding themselves.

With the place so in turmoil, the news was..confusion. This uncertainty is taken with equal seriousness..

'Riff Raff. ' Moley watches, recoils.

Hazards of urban gangs..grow. There's no curfew..yet rules and events shift, preventing any complicity or incipient anarchism. Anticipation. is building

Nervous coughs and a rustling..Someone blurts: 'I needn't waste time.'

Another says as he rumages for a ticket, 'Somethings wrong, who has rights of passage?.'

Duke handles some Keys..The door swings open…He jibes."Lock breaking is mine, Something is tangible, brings disquiet all around."

One person passes past..stumbling, shaken. Another says 'I'm unsure..I almost felt in, but I'll wait here like everyone else for now..'

A sign directs: Private! Guests Only! This way to the Feast.

Byron interrupts: "Sounds possible, why do I always stumble into things..** iT.."

Moley blinks.."Was your..guess that maybe we three- likely as not more are the seventh son of the Seventh.. coincidental? This family thing..items and same apple fallen..chancers of old stooge named Wedgewood. Have you heard - Had a lot of artisans..Made mint, built a name..We all understand performing Brands, status..A dream of a reputation he had.!!"

"Big, with a precipitous ego Wedgewood. Seems right with tiny shrimp underlings - never growing a chance into bigger fishies…" says Duke.

Duke continues.." Must have been kinda imperious don't you think. Probably was a consummate disciplinarian! Keeping order. Georgians are not twenty-first century people ..We've grown too soft..Then you welcomed masters. Apprenticeships lasted lifetimes..Takes respect to give loyalty.."

"What's this? "Byron adds, "These days all we talk about is the past. A golden age! Phaw..Post Eden, Brexit.. and this warren….Why?."

.A strange puckering frown crosses Byron's face." Seems what's missing..Who in this post Apocalypse Island ever eats?? Could you recognise real food..I'm fed up with vitamins and printed protein supplements ….Come to think about it..'Horses, feasts..Something no one in our lifetimes ever seen.!".

A boy appears walking along the middle of the crowd. He is beckoning, getting everyones full attention. The separating crowd hushes,, opening a path.

"I'm Matta. ' Who asks this? How?"

Morley blurts "Is it for real the Feast?"

Matta holds out a long stick and scratches a circle and says "That is what you become.." Duke is beside himself.. "Why?"

Morley: "What brings you, where are you leading us to?"

.Another visitor..asks "You are the inviter. I'm assuming there is an offer or are we all just mistaken?"

Anticipation is building. The crowd grows with other visitors.

They speak of returning..feel this connection..At last being here is home..

Matta intercedes: "I speak of air….That is me..I'm with you. I see rules bring change.."

Matta steers his chalk, skipping as lines dart under nimble feet. His eyes widen, look deeply at everyone.

"Air." He says: "We are breathing, in our hands, inhabiting the world,"

"This is a trial." Matta presses with clear and firmer tones. "You must do everything differently …entering the inner space …Become an entrant into the realm you are shut out of. ""Here you mean?"

By now, there were many more.

"Jury is out "someone said."

"Who says? ' Matta giggles.

The boy is elected to hold out, waiting to meet all for the Party. There's a Feast inside … Matta walks away but stares back.

Like Glass..up against crushing walls..staying invisible, life's ceasing to be real. His playful initiative is what others lack, Real presence, centrality. '

"What right has he….?"

Matta's voice was interceding: "Never shall we ever be overridden."

Something new is afoot, yet the place is a meeting of old precursors.

"We built board games, digital promotions about to happen..What..How frustrating. Morley asks:" Is all against our principles of liberty?"

Matta said 'You are not frosted out..'

"How so?"

The eyes of the audience are getting into the moment..

Everyone watched and saw Matta doesn't get nor claim what they endure.

One in the crowd says "Yes…That City and all becomes..How else, out on a limb, inexcusable

..Dissembling..Breaks me down.."

Matta replies, "I come offering, not starting again. Why must we always be apart, beyond..Incomplete or complaining?"

Matta stood on the other side taking selfies for them to see. He held up his camera, picturing the feast inside, and heralding distorted faces,

'Our right..'

"Yes "one said, "Paid by sweat and diligence …"

Mattas' eyes widened..

"' You cannot claim what is not yours to own …"

Voices, faces grow ugly, mortifying…Angrier …

"You have no Soul..You stand in our way..Let us pass!"

Matta answers …"The Feast is yours.. When your soul comes, the Feast welcomes. All who enjoy it with the greatest appetite - not for anything else- Nothing is more important in this World. Come inside!!!"

ISO-LATION

"If the trousers fit, wear them. He is a stick in the mud. I like the young man though." Old Tarkin nods thoughtfully, looks to the ground.

"Others say 'he can't help it! Has lost his reason in my opinion."

Matt the marine-engineer looks annoyed, scratches his brow." We know quite a bit o'the history! When Pele says "He can't help others, gets left out cos' of it. Or, such is the way if you are a misfit and he can't claw back when you never had anything, no place, home, nor friends. That's stuff 'n nonsense hypocrisy!"

"A fish out of water, can't stay or go…a real problem!" Tarkin shrugs.

Pele, where does he live? The streets, by the river moorings remote for losers and outcasts. He lives on a slip-way, along the Hibernian canal. He can't swim, eats cast off crayfish or fish heads Tarkin puts by Pele's doss next to a kerosene can he sometimes burns all night long. The old oil skin is what covers the skep or coracle he uses.

Tarkin points across to the blue covered bowl, saying "You'll find him one day or night taking sleep or shelter there. I turned it upside down to keep out the cold and rain."

Matt nods. "Better than a tent. Pele was not under it when I went up there, walked past the gypsy vans, the sailmakers hut and the Syrians. They are evil, smoking Ganja, standing around idly, thinking they are something! Are pilferer's, just sicko's, starving to break in."

Tarkin objecting says "No, they don't!"

"They do and I can prove it! Matt scowling, points across to the far row of huts. "Kindra and Pershin's stores were broken into twice last week! They run a tight good service, keeping well stocked provisions for boat parts at short service. We get our tackle from them fast, cost cut. I passed their door last Tuesday just after midnight. Their front door was broken and I heard an uproar, kicking and howling from inside. I went to look and three Syrian…they are not kids saw me, ran past clutching armfuls of food and watches, electronic goods. At first I gave chase, but I went to tell Kindra and Pershin. We spent five hours interviewed by the police."

"These are persecuting times, inflaming strife." Tarkin continues, "Immigrants expect, are still crossing here. Expect something for nothing; it is hard for peaceful people, not outsiders to understand. Pele's father was Mayor of Bradford, organised the August Carnival, and led the kettledrum concert. Humil is a big tall warm guy!"

He say "Feiah- that's what he calls me, We go tomorrow. When I was so small we came here, my brother Jamah and sister Kenya saw only pictures, but I was born in Jamaica and tomorrow I have the tickets and my son Pele comes with me for a long time we go home."

Tarkin screwed up his face in tight concentration. "Humil says 'Why do you look at me like that Feliah? 'I told Humil what I saw and understood. ' You want to know- what-why do you not see this, I told you brother, Pele can't go…'

"Why? "Humil ruffled his bright shirt angrily, and started to pace in the hot evening that late August at the end of the Carnival.

"Because" says Feliah, Pele has troubles and you should speak to him- or else you need as I told you- talk, get it out of him."

Matt "So did they sort it- obviously they never did and I know Humil did not go to Jamaica alone"

Firkin answered, "No, not at first cos' he got into it under the skin, drew out the problem like sly dangerous poison from the troubles - found the time to turn tables, cut away the obfuscations and bit deep into the hide of the gang."

"What was destroying Pele?" Matt asked.

Firkin said "One day he did good, next hit and got ground down by real love problems. It's like this: near where Humil lived was Domo and he has a daughter called Elhelda.

"No!" Matt uttered. "You mean that rich creep, is he a pimp?"

"Elhelda was a real beauty, cute and very smart and never looked at any boys."

Firkin added, "She was only just sixteen at second schooling, was even head girl then. Good at sport, education and was at High school in Bradford. Something got her going cos' Pele's friend Ricky was going out with her best friend Sugar-May and said Pele's smitten he told her how Elhelda looks like his mother. Perhaps she spoke to Domo. I don't know. Pele went to see Domo." Matt: "Domo is a bad guy."

"It's true, Domo's got money and screws up a lot of people, lending money at huge rates.." Firkin added.

"I heard he finishes anyone by fixing them on dope, big time on crack cocaine, if you cut-out of a deal." says Matt.

Firkin: "Domo met Pele I know. He liked the guy, even got his daughter to meet him on one condition. ' You have no chance ever again to even talk, see her, or ever date my only daughter. First you gotta become a man, Pele.' Pele looked crushed. Being seventeen life was all so brilliant and it was the end of the summer term. He told Domo he was going to fly to Jamaica with his father."

"You're not going there" demanded Domo. "Not if you love my daughter. It is a place that will destroy you- is a gangster killing island! Listen-up to me, I have a better prospect for you. If you stay here -promise me not to go, I will help you Big Time with everything, the whole enchilada- riches, my daughter!"

Pele said "Why? I'll talk to you tomorrow."

"Okay "says Domo. "Only come back if you accept my offer."

He returned, ignored his father, never got away on holiday to Jamaica, never even went to the airport.

Pele got to take up with Domo. He pimped, hit on Crack Cocaine, then buried himself in this riverside shanty, to pay back Domo. He never himself thieves, but gets lots of the locals hooked, all hopelessly bailing him and themselves out. They're in a riot, all fixing on his suppliers. The dope he chains with Domo and earns huge money. Most he's gotta pay back.. But never finally can. Pele is a hopeless lost soul; just one pawn inside of Domo's gang.

VW VET

Fidor hated to admit, indeed could not own up how easily he got lost anywhere. His wife Thea is Sat-Nav mad! Chris and Dorthi tagged along all keen, smiles everywhere. Summertime heralded holidays. Dizzy and rattling their sand digging spades, looking for sun, sand, sea and fun.

Fidor had chosen the VW camper named Vet. Why Vet you ask? Fidor saw it six months before. Hidden under tarpaulin used to camouflage tanks prepared for the D-Day landings, the van had been 'mothballed' for over thirty years in his father's garage. Vet he called it, as the old wagon is a veteran vehicle. Vet looked new. Okay, he needed wheels and Vet had yet to get serviced on the road for the holiday.

Vet and Fidor just got on. Getting so breezed, I got all in the best of moods. Soon the Vet was gone! All eager, like a kite above water, the trail felt like a treck from an old western. Tipping his sombrero over his eyes, Fidor gripped tightly, knowing these reins held-up, leading Fargo's horses to the drink.

Vet and Thea saying her "Gotten-Dammerings' ', all the way made the first stop at Bognor Regis, arriving finally at EastBourne on the fourth day. A mixed bag for road brakes and stop-overs, buying keepsakes or adding to family albums, re-routing for links and pastimes.

Fidor argued with Zim, his father, about who was 'in', who was 'out'. Who lived or else had died or left the country. Likewise, Thea had two-penny worth of arguments.

"Let's include Elthreda, Bethada, or Belza and Sandy! We can't forget them on this visit!" Thea tirelessly went through old diaries and five address books, looking for phone numbers and newer addresses. She added to her long lists the "Differs and the Singleton's..And old Bathne' Shake! Fred and the rest of their clan...Sure that is the last one!"

All these cousins, wanting...She scratched her head remembering Fred's valedictions, "You must call on us!"

Fidor shrugged, "They're on-route, fifth removed or seven times related..!"

"We will need a removal van." These words shook sleep from Fidor, He got the holiday arranged, excavating Vet from under all that dust.

That summer the Motorway exceeded, with tailbacks and holdups following nature's call. Further stops as ice ran out and sudden downpouring rain brought tail-backs. Rallying sounds of swallows or views of fluttering yachts, milling in harbour mouths, eventually thinned out longest queues.

On such a bounty of promises the family were led by Vet streaming forwards, while Fidor coasted, always in denial to the Sat-Nav and Thea's navigating blandishments..

The family arrived! Bonnet and boot doors lifted together. Chin took out his menagerie. Spotting the beach before everyone, he clambered with the wooden zoo of animals, hastening to assemble a maze of sand lodgings before the lapping waves.

Struggling into the chalet with the bags, Fidor checked into the porti loo. In a tin out-building, this was a WW11 Anderson shelter. Thea went off for fresh water. Forty feet from the front, the Chalet consisted of a small kitchen-diner and two bedrooms.

Thea's Grandpa emerged from the kitchen at Bogner, carrying a samovar. One sherbet cake and tiers of crab sticks, muffins and Moldovian popsicles. Then, adding further consolation for the holiday reconciliation, from the rear closet burst Beth and Clarissa, two of their Great Aunts! They choursed "Welcome! Welcome!" They had big garlands of fresh gardenias and baskets of rose petals they profusely flung over Thea, Fidor and Pring the Basset hound!

Barefoot or with buskins, Fodor's feet usually conformed in office leathers, quickly acclimated to the shales and hot sands. The haze of heat shone over Vet, parked to the roadside, next to the sea dunes. Teeming native castaways and thronging holiday makers spilled from arcades and hotels. Bobbing like corks or jellyfish, surfers and snorkelers bubbled or scorched actively upon the streaming waves. Arcades and bars spewing with ferry goers and wayfarers shipped and spewed out from bar to bar. The afternoon tilted forwards toward dusk; unzipping light and hanging her costumes out drying…

Threaded local sardines fizzled, hissing on the smouldering barbeques piling up onto plates of laden salads. Seafoods made an exquisite garnish for their tea. Suddenly darkness erupted with festive lights! Flaming furores of fireworks burst starlights over them as they sat eating. After the last display, the sea and sky turned dismal and grey; darkness surrounded them again. That night, Thea bathed as black closed in. The children and Pring slumbered, rolled to bed.

That night a shark appeared. Over the sides of his bed, Fidor's legs dangled. Inky fluorescence lit up the subterranean landscapes in blooms of emerging forests. The vegetation cascaded alive.

Under flickering eyelids, Fidor slipped into the seat of Vet and drove. With no destination in his sights, the camper sped away. Behind him, his family were stranded. Rising sea-life surged and cast higher, lapping forwards along the coastal ledges. A great white predator grew near, emboldened by the tidal flowing fastnesses surging upwards. Prominent by a shining white scarred nose, one intent shark charged forwards, followed by a whole shoal scenting hapless holiday sleepers…

Thea awoke at the earliest time. The sun pinged already at 5am. The chalets tiles were already hot! Pring was outside sniffing in the bin for fish tails. She said, "Where is Fidor?" She then realised she was alone! She asked herself, "Where are you, children!?"

Thea looked eastwards…She cupped her hands before the sharp sunlight, expecting to see Vet. Of course, the vehicle was there, but looking luckless, different now as it lay over on its side. Thea walked over and was shaken. Vet was completely wrecked! Vet's body had been cut open, as if sliced by a giant cleaver. Just then, behind her, her husband appeared. He looked very dishevelled and awful.

Fidor said, "What a nightmare I had!"

Thea exploded, "Where have you been? Where are the children!?!"

Fidor held Thea close to him…"They are here…They' re quite safe!" .

They both looked behind. Sure enough, the children were running about as usual, chasing each other!

With eyes shining fiercely bright, Fidor spoke. "I must tell you..I saw a ghost! The van, Vet and I…We were driving all night…it fought for Eastbourne, all the holiday makers here! You slept Thea, didn't you? We were attacked by hordes of sharks…So many there were, it is unbelievable!"

Fidor fell to his knees. "Last night so many sharks came for us, sweeping up to the beach. How, Why? We escaped!"

As he shook, Fodor's eyes widened. Spasmodically his mouth quivered in sheer horror. "Vet, drove like a maniac, was compelled to meet them..these sharks! Vet's conviction was absolute , so real! Vet sensed the terror and the overwhelming threat from these sharks I tell you! The van, Vet, ran aground. We fought them and the teeth…Ahhh, all those thrashing mouths foaming, with cuts and red blood streaming followed …!"

Overwhelmed by memory now, Fidor stopped. Pausing by the shock of forces hitting him back . He added, "Those sharks just kept on coming!"

Thea clasped her husband tightly to her as Fidor continued. "They really charged like hungry wolves, breaking into us. As they drove us back here…they tore us in half! The metal body of Vet screamed as did those sharks! Vet, by God how he fought! Like a great zip, Vet ate them. He was chewing all of those gnashing murderous sharks up!"

Fodor's body bent right over, shaking in anger, pain and triumph. All his terror he let out, saying finally, "Vet saved us. Then, although he died, I know it sounds impossible, Vet is our hero, he brought us through!"

DIAMONDS

The last flour disappeared through the sieve. On his lip the bite was hard, bringing blood. He thought 'how easy it is to swear revenge. Once I had nothing before yesterday's good fortune. Today again I have nothing'

It was his family he cared for now. But though Brinklovs' wife, sister and mother had no wish to ignore him, they had no choice for this Judas, but to turn away. So they said nothing; voluble were the black looks from their backs. Another curtain had been drawn.

Kruinov, the Balkan Prefector had proven malefactor, yet swore as proving turncoat to Brinklov, that it was he who had defectors allegiances. Brinklov had upheld open Democratic government. He held his ground as the shootings and imprisonments of the people began. When he stood up to it, he was told 'run traitor, or else be shot!'

An era of extortion, money changers, black-mail and subversions set in. Families fled and were hunted down across minefields. Some resorted to smuggling out endangered men, equally risking their own precious lives. Security was rented apart. Elmeira, Brinklovs mother, sought to save him. For three terrifying days he hid in the house basement.

Finally she said "Go now. Leave, it is night. I have arranged for you to meet a helper. In a houseboat she sits alone, waiting to meet you. Walk to the river Tsaltin, thirty miles south of here, from the outskirts of Boulketan city. She, the widow of Cossack Russ has contacts; shall guide you from out of this misfortune."

Knowing the scent of murderers at his tail, the rat grows cunning. Shooting down all available bolt holes for cover at the faintest sounds and shadows from swiveling machine gun towers.. Brinklov made a frisson from all these haunting changes.

In Kruinovs office, no secret was made over rapid recruitments of spies. Zealots under duress of death got ample rewards within the circle of his forged manacles of tightening steel.

Madam Creschewn was and remained a Chetchyn with Mongolian sympathies. She sat beautiful but passively before a deep aquarium, filled with snakes and poisonous crustaceans and fish.

"There are few" she demurred, "bitterer than I. Like these snakes in brine, I am left as lifeless upon the lowest rungs, made impoverished by these fascist gluttons. I'll help you my comrade friend, of course… But first" she said huskily, we make love!"

"Nothing comes without its legacy." The Chetchyn leader Prochav knew his tactics were oppressed, therefore limited. "You stay with us in these mountains for how long.. He shrugged, "enough."

He continued,"Until we get you to safety in the west, hey Brinklov? We move on up now. The Chetshyn fighter never, never ever rests. Only between moments of movement. We have much action yet, how do you say..

He laughed, "To pacify the stupid Balkan Russian enemies. They die weaker than wasps before the real cold sets in. These teeming stupid flies.

We are tigers; a dead Russian gives us appetite! Vollah. But we save and dispense our ammunition wisely. Mostly we use up the wasted enemies!" Eager for blood, the fighting though fast was very ferocious. On both sides surprise action occurred, at the crack of dawn or before dusk. The Chetchyns' pursued the Russians' like predatory eagles baiting carrion.

Madam Creschewn said "That is better!" She had raw, crude but brilliant laughter. "We are laid bare. The Russians are under Kruinov; our beloved Balkans are pillaged. But we never give up our fleece of diamonds! We are too proud and cunning for that."

She added, "The flow of blood drains from their own cut throats, poisoning their own sacred waters. And like me, no true person stands long to be crucified. They are venal, puerile savages. All of them!"

A terrifying thought hit Brinklov, seared by the mountainous winds. 'Men are born and die between these ricocheting bullets, the mind thwarting barbed wires enclosing him!'

Yet something else he witnessed, there were women fighters tending children and elderly, the sick and the dying. Cooking and nursing routinely, with women victims.

He remembered a long holiday in Iceland five years before, watching the skuas diving for fish. Here Russian men tortured the Chetchyn, then buried them up to their necks. Planted with undetonated grenades in their rifle butted mouths.

Like skuas, he felt they were roped together, one by one falling into a black chasm-like conduit of entrapment. The Chetchyn recoiled upwards for a moment. Another dead Russian engorged in their mouths.

The two armies clashed, flinging together in embattled weight, their flailing fists. Brinklov, pincered at the rear phalanx, moved exhausted as the Chetchyn's advanced stealthily. Sharp and united into an machine-like arrowhead, they grouped pointedly disciplined,.

The answer to how they were sustained came soon enough. They had solidly marched through the Ullgarin pass for three days without rest, along a narrow river valley.

Prochov said "We rest here until first light. Below us, a half-kilometre away is the Russian enclave. I need ten volunteers to go now!"

Brinklov felt crazed with weariness but hurriedly agreed. The Chetchyn fighters almost fought themselves for a place. In their earnest appetite to fight, they passionately turned on Prochov. He screamed orders.

"Have no pleasure but to kill. If you fail, all are denied fruits of battle, the filthy fill of spoils."

Armed to the teeth and stripped to the waist, they all themselves smeared totally in black howitzer grease. Their single razor sharpened bayonet reflected no light. Forty-six Chetchyns stayed behind. The descent was hindered by deeper snow. As the path levelled, their pre-attacking strategy emerged. They split into five groups of twos: to work, staying together.

Prochov went first with Brinklov. He hissed: "Stick close, each must kill a Russian! I slit the throat. You fill the sack with food and ammunition. Together. Me then you, and vice-versa."

There had been much discussion, strategies, and well rehearsed tactics. There stood the first sentry watch. Bolstered large by his great-coat, slowly swinging his body clockwise in his bolt hole.

Our swift approach had tracked, then mapped the conscripts from their rear. Prochov's stealth brought him the prize, Together they leapt. Silently the severed victims fell. Prochev worked fast: cursing as he felled the soldier.

"Brinkov, pass the sack." He quickly filled it with two kalashnikovs and a small wallet of rubles. One hundred metres along, Brinkov too lunged, falling upon his sentry. Prochov barked "Enough. The Russians are running off pell mell out of camp.

He added, "They have no guts. We too must leave."

They regrouped. "Brinkov, it's in the bag. You are a hero!"

Prochov showed the sentries head, holding it up by the hair. Brinkov protested, but his horror and protest was ignored.

Prochov said "We had the pigs by the curlies. Well done."

The ten all returned, having leapt like eager wolves, each pair taking out two or more Russians, returning to camp with loaded spoils. It was shared out with the rest; black bread aplenty, salted beef and a coveted prize.

"We killed a General." They had braids. For only one of that rank would have possessed three bottles of vodka, six boxes of Puskin cigars and three precious sealed jars of Moldavian black caviar.

It was to be Brinkov's first and last sortie. Prochov had received fresh orders. Brinkov had been told of his further value.

"The Russians offer us freedom for an exchange! It is rubbish these offers. This filthy freedom, pa! Nothing. I tell them.

There was an airlift. Madam Creschewn had seen to that. As promised, her words: "I move in high circles" were so.

Prochov had taken Brinkov higher. His cards, played always close to his chest, made the Chetchyn fighters withdraw higher into the encircling peaks. For them, it was a fiercely uncertain time.

Then Prohov said "We as fighters set great store in ridding our country of all Russians. We must continue our war. We must send you away to London as our Democratic ambassador!"

He laughed and continued, "Madame Creschewn, she has paid for the flight, with perhaps her own life! All of Russia has been talking; their mailers have such interminable passions. In the Winter Palace, they have her black diamonds already on display.

He added, "She slyly lied, giving her word of their loan, to 'send Brinkov home.' She has told me, each is triggered to explode into a gigantic firework display when you are gone, one month from today."

SPLIT-AFFINITY

In the field's expanses, the cropper's beacons briefly turned and swung out wide as they rolled over the prairie. Flies and dust arose on the thrashing cutters. Swiftly the broad spidery arms were drawing under the ripe waiting corn.

Out behind the fifth harvester, the fitter's dog Malchin, a brown deer hound, returned. A limp rabbit dropped next to his truck. Sleek and eager, the dog ran off again into the darkness. He ran past the trucker's post, with his nose still down, sweeping. On the next report of the beater's guns, he turned.

Minchin's legs had just crossed back from the field's edge when another lone gun went off. A smoking barrel emerged from a single cropper's small white caravan. That dog's body blew right back into uncut corn.

With field dirt and flies, half of the net covering the caravan door was grimy and torn. The other side was tightly held, pulled back by the outstretched cropper's boot. Half asleep, his right eye still lit upon the smoking, breached gun glinting in the shadows. His right hand tightly held an important letter crumpled and dirty, the cropper had carried, reread for the last thirty years.

Earlier that evening there'd been a harvester's party. Already the croppers were on their last week. Arny Beech had had a good season. On this Saturday as foreman of this rookie bunch he'd addressed them. He said, "You drovers are punch lucky. I kinda respect you. And we've not stopped going, but for this evening's break.

The only one time let me remind you we did, was that freak of nature. When that Vancouver typhoon hit us...!" The hundred men, all agreeably cheered, hearty after several beers.

Arny continued, "Any how's, we've sure got the corn cumin' in. A fine yield I'll add! And I'd like to treat ye all to four rounds each. That is of course on top of the coming wages and this year's special bonus!"

J smiled wryly. He'd just been voted 'king roller' for the third consecutive year. Barely clasping his magnum of bourbon on two drunken legs, he loudly shouted. "Arny, you're a' sure mother fucker! Me an' us boys just' want to' thank you for gettin' us all through ag'in"

J's was the best fitter in the line. Working ceaselessly, he kept engines and parts smoothly flowing. Never dropping out when breakdowns threatened to snarl up the run. A seasonal worker like the resty J's was more than reliable.

Regarding their own uncharted histories, to them J's was the same. "In season, that's most of summer, he's a very sour son of a bitch. As all the rest, J's a hobo after. Seasonally we're out o' work. When us roadies cut off back 'n t' town...

Somehow J's clung on. He told noone but the chief fitter Greg his problems and sometimes Greg's dog Malchin. This season Greg's temper had blackened. While usually affable as apple-pie, he'd turned to drinking heavily. Making his heavy debts worse. "I'm sure afraid Mary's left me. An' now I'm certain, I'm gonna' lose the house. J's, please, I'm sorry again to ask...". Greg owed J's from last season.

Over and over the fixations. J's reread his uncle's letter. It read:

"Your father Eron spent his late years bed ridden. His legs had been clammed-up in callipers after being trapped. Last from out the pit, the whole mining community had given him up, like those other poor bastards sure left for dead."

Sometimes he wore a welded iron cage for straightening up his torn and crippled spine. It did little good. He was in agony. Used to being the fittest, working more overtime than most. His pride was in working, cutting new seams of coal below four thousand feet in Minnesota's heartlands.

"Your mother Mira's love was in the home. Before Eron's fall she had twins. They'd told me they'd just about lost any hope in having children. She spent all her time on them, nursing and running off to the hospital. Both herself and the boys were sickly".

"Eron grew angry. He'd go into prolonged rages without her unbroken attention. Used as he was to only be having her for himself. He took to drinking in a big way. Also, to gambling, then having fights and wandering away from home at night. Some said he'd got another woman. I don't think he had. That was his way in trying to adjust" Just before he died, someday he went back. Mira was with only one child. Eron said to me, he'd asked Mira:

"Where's the other boy Mira?" She never answered him, only shook her head. That was all he ever got by way of a proper explanation"

"We like to remember our past here". The journalist's blue eyes sparkled. "I'll remember to put that line in I'll promise you! Do you know our newspaper is out Friday? Sure, we've been right round this great new place. What was the kiddies Home like, 'The Reaches' before the fire destroyed it?"

Joe answered, "Why, you'll have to speak to somebody else, I wasn't in charge then..."

The journalist shrugged, "I'm sorry, I thought you were somebody else".

He was looking intently at Joe's lapel badge. I just noticed your initials, J.S. printed on the door. "Wasn't the previous director called Julian Simons?"

Joe smiled, correcting this mistake, "I'm Joseph. I prefer Joe Sego. Mr. Simon perished in that terrible fire..."

Warmly he offered the journalist his hand. Suddenly he laughed. "I'm so sorry, I didn't quite catch your name. Ah yes, Bob! Of course! Why, my colleagues, they tell me you know the old hands here. There are so many helpers from old families, each sharing names going back generations. being thirty though, I'm about the youngest in place here"

Bob said "thank-you, that explains so much. I'll be off then. I'll maybe call back if I want some more details!"

Joe, diffident as usual said, "Glad to be helpful. Sometimes it does feel like deja vu here. I once came here as a boy. There was a traveling circus on the grounds. I visited it with my parents long ago.

"Roll up, roll up. Come on all, let's have a go…" The memories flooded back. The side man eagerly heaved forwards off his stool. His fat hands held two coconuts up towards them. Joseph stood between two elders. Looking eager, he seemed firmly held back in their grasp. "I'll get them Mira" he shouted, rushing forwards.

As the small hands reached up, the man, wearing callipers, lunged behind the boy. With the full force of his hand, he hit him on the back of his head. Instantly, Joe crashed to the ground, sprawling at the seller's feet.

The woman screamed out, "Oh don't Eron, Joe's only playing".

But Eron replied, "Why Mira, he's getting out of hand, wait 'till I get him home!"

Joe saw the brawny face of the coconut man frowning angrily. His right hand twisted up, undercutting Eron's chin. He shouted "That's for hitting the boy".

Eron staggered with eyes closed. Dropping forwards, he then fell half on his knees. But Eron had a miner's strength. An ugly fight ensued. The fat seller fared worse. Heavier than showering coconuts, he got pile-drivers fists hitting him.

Mira took Joe off to the magic mirror's tent, saying "You'll enjoy the funny figures. You go right in son. I'll stay out if you don't mind. I'm just going to sit here for a little while and take some air".

As Joe entered, he saw a young man coming towards him, walking upside down. His hands were waving in the air and his body floated strangely upon them. 'I rushed past it, turning to the right and this figure disappeared. Even quicker, I then met another before me. Yet as I peered up, to catch a proper glimpse of his face, he grew taller than a house! Wearing clothes like mine, amusingly his head was just pea sized. I ran towards the other mirrors, realising it was a game'

'I met again a figure first looking like me. As I moved, shapes jumped out, grew more distorted. I saw something different was happening here. These shapes motioned and danced. And had a life of their own. Shaking in the image, another appearance was emerging. I knew it was not myself! Staring back, disturbing and weird, was another's face. Before me, quite divorced from my own reflection, the boy independently waved at me! My mind's memory connected. I saw my lost identical brother'

"It's J's". He uttered a silent message. "I'm alive!" The face darkened and then disappeared.

Outside, I found my mother lying in a faint upon the ground. I felt frightened. She was so pale and shivering. She whispered, "Call an attendant, the red cross is here. I'll go to the hospital. I'll be fitting soon, father's gone with the police. Take this". Mira handed Joe a piece of paper detailing the police's phone number. She added, "When I go to hospital, you return home. Call them. Tomorrow, visit me. I'll be ok. Tell me the news".

That night, a new fate befell Joe. He rang the police. Sergeant Horne said, "Speak up boy, I can hardly hear you. Joe. What is it you want? You say you're ringing about Eron. There must be a mistake. Revil. Oh Yes. That's his surname! Well, he got here drunk and he's been sick. In our cell he is for safety. I'll ring you back soon. I'll tell him you've called and tell you how he's doing"

Joe waited for that call. His eyes stung with tears watching the seconds hand on his watch. He stayed by the phone patiently for three hours. So long, he felt quite ill himself and nauseous with worrying over his mother in hospital.

Torn between leaving or staying in the house, finally Joe ran the two miles to the hospital.

Arriving at the information desk, a nurse escorted Joe up to casualty. There he met with a doctor called Mr Hazez. He spoke softly, yet his face wore a precise expression of fixed gravity. He tried to be friendly, but solemnity was in his eyes.

"J's isn't it? I have been with your mother. We have met before, you and your mother. One month ago, she came to us when she had fallen down. She needed our help to get well. J's, I must tell you. This time it has been much worse for her. Now she is so seriously ill, she has gone into a coma. I am so very sorry to tell you this J's. She will be safe with us. You are tired".

The doctor called for a soft drink of juice for Joe.

He continued speaking, "I understand you are alone now at home. A policeman rang here a quarter of an hour ago. You were trying to find out about your father Eron. Please try not to be frightened. There is some sad news to tell you. The police surgeon says your father had been drinking before going into custody. He became sick and vomited, causing him to choke. Despite all the best attempts, he stopped breathing. They attempted many times resuscitation, but he died"

The doctor's staring eyes swelled. Joe could see nor listen any longer. He covered his head in his hands. Tears ran overwhelming. The rawness grasped at his stomach, chilling up his heart. Filling up him with dread and desolation. Grief sunk in as Joe focused on the news.

The doctor took up the phone. He rang a number and spoke. "I have a young man with me. He is ten years old. Yes, just ten. He needs a place for the night. Can you help please? You can. Good! Please come along as quickly as you can and pick him up. I'll tell him and explain what this is all about".

"You have to be with people Joe," said Mr Hazez "A man is coming from a home called 'The Reaches', where you will stay until we see what happens with your mother". He went on to explain that this is the law; having to be there for safety.

When Joe arrived at the home he was greeted by the matron, a beaming faced, stout women. She introduced herself as "Cauldwell, call me Sue. I've some very sad news I'm afraid. Your mother Miras passed away an hour ago. She didn't suffer…

Joe screamed "You're all bloody liars! The Dr, Mr Hazez. I've only just left him. He said she was alive". He sobbed, "You're in league with the Police, to stop me being at home with my parents. Eron is too strong, he'd never choke like this. He can't be gone! I'll never stay sister. I'd rather burn or rot in hell than stay here!"

Joe's agony deepened. At night he had endless nightmares. Sue featured strongly as Dracula's handmaiden. In his bedroom was a long mirror. In this appeared his twin, saying "You're not alone Joe, I'm here to rescue you". Before and after he had gone, flames appeared.

Not before long Joe doubted he would ever be rescued by J's.

There certainly was something familiar but disturbing about J's.

Joe shouted, "leave me alone! You're the devil tormenting me!" He began blaming J's his twin with everything, all the bad fate and ill fortune now befalling him.

Yet the voice and face of J's did not leave. In fact, it grew closer and its message more insistent. "Look around you. I know we both share the same conscience. How can I force you to reject this life? To unshackle yourself from the suffering around you?" As J spoke Joe felt J's hot breath burning away the air, scorching at his own face.

He saw more and more the suffering of the other children, inflicted by the carers. Joe overheard visitors being turned away. Bad neglect was all around. Faeces littered the floor. Carers fought and clawed them with their fists. J's message of anger to Joe grew into a flame of burning revenge.

Before the smoke, Joe saw fire. The flames, like huge molten candles, swam along the bottom of the dormitory door. Curling up the paint work, they joined and ignited together. Joe heard the siren. The sounds of breaking glass. And the belting, scrunching sounds of running feet. Voices were shouting "the ladders, go higher. Fetch more ambulances".

Around Joe were choruses of curdling, piercing screams. "I'm burning, help me someone! For God sakes, the rooms are all in flames!"

As Joe scrambled through the heat and choking thick smoke, down the corridor he came face to face with the arsonist, Joe saw him carrying a splashing can smelling of petrol. His face was quite burnt after inhaling the smoke and hot flames.

A terrible chill hit Joe despite the raging fire. He said "Why, it's J's…My twin…" Grinning maniacally as he glanced and nodded, J returned back the stare. As always, J's was running now. Joe suddenly realised that it was him who'd started the fire.

He shouted, "Like for you Joe, others had closed their hearts and doors on me. Yet I've got even. You're even more twisted-up, with hatred Joe. Left burning-up here!" Then he gave a horrid, pitiless laugh.

Nobody laid any accusations on him. Joe had a long convalescence after the fire. He had good plastic surgery for his terrible first-degree burns. He got satisfaction too in knowing he could choose his identity. Making good his destiny. First thing though he resolved when well enough, to track down J's.

Joe searched for ten years. He drew a line through all the J's, selecting carefully then eliminating the phone names from Oklahoma to Tennessee. Sometimes he almost got a convincing sighting. While Joe's surgery had taken well, J's hadn't had any surgery. In the fire he was shocked by J's contorted limbs. His right face was still scarred.

Joe spoke to a doctor, confiding to him his motives. "I come out every summer here to the mid-west just hoping, searching to meet

The doctor looked shrewdly at Joe. "It occurs to me" he said, that you are suffering from selective hysterical syndrome"

Taken aback by this, Joe answered "What do you mean?"

"Well," he said, "You are incurable. I know you as two halves of the same man. To you, the other one, this 'J's' who really died, lives on. It is all a crazy fantasy! Only you refuse to recognise this fact… You are convinced he has assumed a hidden identity. That perhaps he is working now on a farm or under a false passport. To you he assumes another alias, then goes on long journeys aboard a ship…"

Joe was angry, feeling these comments to be very intrusive. But he shrugged his shoulders. "Well, whatever you are saying doc, I know it's more than this. Where before J's would appear as just himself, I am now convinced he's trying to change his identity. To convince me into believing he's somebody else. Meanwhile I'll keep on searching. I'm getting near the truth"

The doctor said "It's as I say, I can't really help you. Maybe," he said smiling, "your paths already cross. All you really have in your possession is fear. You make up a story to resolve something hidden in your own past. You then tell me that this stranger is seeking you out… That just maybe he is eager to get on, to square with you". The doctor's eyes smarted in jubilation, showing humour. He said emphatically, "It's crap."

Joe's anger was palpable. He rounded on the doctor, grabbing tightly at his throat lapel. He hissed, shaken. Both eyes were rolling and clouding over: "Doctor beware I say, beware!"

KNOT OF GRAILECH

I am Dolan, an Armagh man, brought up to philter ponies. Yes horse trading and doctoring before the regIstration of laws and animal rights stamped heinous legitimacy to everything. My brother Fillian, two years older, was in the Sinn Finn territorials, in Ulster. For many years we grew up apart except at key critical times when at Christmas, or marches or funerals - we would shake hands, wink with uproarious laughter over crackers: we are not, never are conversationalists.

Our lines and undertows of contact collided somehow together. When I failed my veterinarian exams my wife Shelly won through, so our farm got certificated, specialising in old and ill horse infirmities and health problems. The generation's knowledge of shoeing and plant lore was second nature and natural to me. Politics, especially the 'Troubles' of IRA and Northern Ireland impinged only as a small notional pinprick when Fillian stepped over my threshold that evening 8 months ago in June. He looked red, tanned. I knew he was in trouble as he wore a beret and smelt of cordite.

"How tidy, organised here your place is brother Dolan…."

He asked me to stay as he admitted 'home life' was worrying, getting rather tough. I sensed this was critical and an understatement. Did Fillian know what really was afoot or how much of a problem he was in, he would not explain. I offered my help and he shook my hand.

"That's a promise."

We both simultaneously spoke. Our folks connect, bind and call this the 'Knot of Grailech.'

Fillian holed up till the right signal. I heard him in the early hours at 3am on the phone. Still wearing a Para uniform, his back was turned to me speaking Gael-Irish. I caught several words: 'trap'..and ' I am ready', 'alone', ' shoot to kill ', and the reminder of 'ransom money ' and what must be paid and 'his debts.' Yet before that morning I could contest or engage with Fillian, he disappeared.

Shelly said "I can get help, this place is running well enough. She implored me to get away. Her hands shook as the boiled eggs toppled into the egg cups. Her blue eyes filled with tears. Like me, she loves Fillian. Then she said" I must tell you, the whisperers know and I underline this, "more than one life is at stake here. There are high stakes, big debts and when you go as you must, both you and Fillian may be gone for a very long time…"

Dolan had read the Northern Irishman headlines, "Gunman gets away, Northern Minister shot Dead!"

Only Dolan knows with a true informers knowledge what really he must do, and where he has to go, for the 'Grialech' is the way of horse whisperers: protecting with fealty those who concur to their own kith. He took an early train to the capital Belfast, then walked due north, leaving the outskirts of the city far out into the remote countryside, walking until it grew dark.

Dolan sensed as he stepped over three stiles he was on the right path. Both behind him the sounds of horses and in front of him grew louder, nearer.. Then before darkness closed in, he was surrounded by a great gathering of horses. Dolan looked down. Under him was fresh soil and the breathing of a grey horse whispered "Here lies your brother Fillian."

Dolan stopped then knelt. His right hand entered the soil and touched the body, then closed the others, held the hand of his brother and as he had expected, Fillian had enough left to clench Dolan.

"This pact" said the whisperer "is for ourselves and for you, The Grailech.' You Dolan have taken on a burden that must be repaid. Both of you to have life must forfeit everything, to get back you must repay."

Fillian at that moment suddenly sat up like a zombie. His chest had a massive hole where his heart had sat and his whole body was whiter, stiffer than marble. The grey horse spoke again, "Now you have tied your knot, given your love, Fillian will turn to dust and you Dolan will also go away. Fillian is your brother and through you, he will get a new life, after your wife Shelly fulfils her part…"

The greys muzzle close upon his neck blew warm air. "Dolan, you must come with me, mount up now."

The withers of the grey whitening in seamless exertion flew over mountains, never slowing until its hooves touched the outskirts of Dublin. Then the grey spoke again. "Take from my saddle your brother Fillian's heart. You must go across the street to the house in front of you. I wait for you Dolan. Knock once…"

After an hour walking down a tree lined road, the weeping sound from the shoulder bag so upset Dolan he felt relieved when finally reaching the house. As his fist hit the door an adjacent giant casement next to it flew open. A short red headed woman and two muscle-bound henchmen on either side all pointed at Dolan.

"Drop and open the bag!"

Fillian lifted up and opened the contents onto the ground. First rolled out the head of the minister, then beside was the bleeding heart of Fillian, still wailing. Fillian's distinctive voice said, "Here is the money I forfeited for your life and lost my own..is that not enough?"

Finally from the bag fell the ransom money in grubby and torn sheaths of Republican punts.

The decapitated Minister blurted, spitting blood and venom. "Curses, curses, CURSES! Money, life! What good are they? We are now broken, lying here BUSTED! I tell you to do what must be done, curse Fillian! Go to hell Dollan!"

Dolan stood aghast, then took to his racing heels. The red headed wife to the Minister and her gunmen shouted, "Blast him!" and again, "Revenge is the answer!!!", "Kill…Kill Him!"

The guns burst open…fire cracking bullets exploded at his burning feet…Dolan snatched up the bag and carried off Fillian's heart.

A year passed. No news from Dolan returned to Shelly except the whispers had grown stronger.

"Something is happening…"

On the night of the anniversary Shelly had kept awake. Tinkling sounds of china shivering in the kitchen had woken her…Then came stronger sounds from far away…hooves moving, coming from the north slowly running in the distance towards her. So clearly they echoed that Shelley looked out. As she strained her eyes searching for movements in the dark she saw a great grey horse carrying a man, whose silhouette stirred her…

"Dolan, is that you?!"

StarIng so expectantly, Shelly's bright hopes stayed even as the horse and rider disappeared. Shelley finally washed and dressed and peered from her kitchen towards the birthing paddock. Two small newly born black ponies had arrived, already able to jerk and jump. Their umbilical cords kept them tethered, so hobbled.

Shelley rushed outside to help…Had she time to hear…In her head came another voice, whisperings.. "You must cut this tie. Only then will Dolan and Fillian come back to you..!"

BOLIP^E

Bolip^e has no mother. Before he was born his father Rulhu left for war. His Auntie Eb^e looks after him, but is dying in the parlour. She has ebola.

Santi Medecins du Monde frontier base is three miles from here, in a remote village north of Kinshasa in West Africa. Bolip^e is missing. He used to attend school. On the roll call, his address is recorded: they check him but only find his lifeless Aunt Eb^e. Where is he? Kob^e, the medical officer, meets with the school head Timja. Kob^e says "He may already have ebola! Start your search straight away!"

Bolip'e has a cousin named Masha, looking after the homestead. When Eb^e, his Auntie died, Bolip^e ran to the mountains looking for Masha. When Masha had not seen Bolep^e, he asked the elders in the village. "Is Bolip^e safe?"

"The school he attends has got him, he's in quarantine."

Bolip^e knew such fear, he ran. For the child missed most of all his mother Mahla. The daughter of a farmer, she had milked the cows, herded them to market. Bolip^e felt safe, having always lived with animals. Now he hid out in the fields. He drank the milk of the pregnant ewe after her lamb was still born. They live closely together.

Masha's youngest brother Tabu, with his ancient father Mahli milks the sheep and cows, tending and droving. Masha goes out with the search party West of Sierra Leone. He walks five miles to Kozo, to the farmstead where Mahla had once lived.

He stood over her grave, remembering how she had died at only twenty, saving her herd. When marauder's had broken in, shooting her as she fought to defend them. Silently he waited by her grave. In him, he saw her face. The voice, distinctly gentle, is Mahla. "Go home.

Bolip^e is safe. Take care of your animals."

Here, all around Kinshasa and Sierra Leone, in all the monstrous heat, ways familiar, old freedoms were dissolving. Timj'e met Masha in his school's office and Masha told of his visit to Kozo.

"The presence of ancestors there is strong. I tell you, Mahla is alive!"

Timj'e said "Masha, you must stay away now. You must wash yourself all over and stay clean. Then go back home." He pointed out of the window "Look, it is a curfew here!"

Outside, blue-suited men were taping off the streets, spraying roads and verges assiduously, sterilising the centre of the town. "The mortuary is full and the school is shut." Timj'e wept.

"Heartlands are becoming wastelands," Aki announced. At bright noon, beneath the cool Baobab trees where until recently the elders met and prayed, the stooping vultures congregated, all cackling. "I hear their consternation, the ancestors, even they are bewildered! "said Aki.

The vulture 'Grey hooded one' or Tumo with the bulging red gorged beak let out a guttural trumpeting blast. "Gone today is good! Far enough and fast, for young or old, the Veldt is purified. We have never tasted so much flesh! And before some die, we help them on their way!"

A shot rang out - SHABANGGG...The bloated birds in turmoil rose up, railing in sweltering motion - flapping awkwardly up and away, to go from the blasting noise.

Masha stayed on, helping with the search party for ten more days. He was ascribed to be with four groups, sent out to secure and check surrounding lands. Every other day they went out wearing protective suits, carrying sprays of powerful antiseptics and stretchers for the sick or dead. Also, they put up posters for advice, warnings displayed 'Keep At Home', 'Wash Your Body And Keep Your Homes Clean', and to 'Cook All Foods.' The digging burials was hardest - the sick were brought into the new camp hospitals run by military NGO's.

Tabu and Mahli awoke from their mats. The animals were restless, yet it was still dark. Tabu heard something unusual above the coursing, tumbling river noises- he strained his eyes to see. Mahli joined him, held his shoulder - pointed across, over the far bank. "Look" Tabu shouted, "It is Masha! There is something wrong with him!" Masha sat slumped over. Uttering a low feeble pained cry, twisting his head, he was struggling to breathe. "He has the fever" said Mahli.

"Bolip^e "whispered Masha, "I know he's safe, his mother spoke to me..!"

Tabu and Mahli gathered Masha onto a bed next to the river and bathed him with clean fresh water, to cool his weak feverish body. For three days and three nights they fed him, bathing Masha constantly, holding his head up above the river's surface, to purge the surfaces of all contamination. Then, a ewe, the one that Tabu found, that lost it's first born, brings Masha her lost lamb's milk.

Many months had passed. Mahli wiped Masha's eyes. Tabu worked with Masha, everyday growing stronger. "Eboli", Mahli uttered measured, resigned words, "Has taken away so much, but you Mashi and Yes, Bolip^e are still here today!"

Bolip^e had opened his mouth for the first time when the ewe gave up her precious milk to Masha. Tearing himself from under the ewe, he stood naked, like a first born before Tabu and the prostrating figure of Masha.

"That fortune's face changed everything!" remarked Masha, recalling how the small figure of Bolip^e had broken the torment of the beleaguering fever, dulling all his sapping hope. Masha's eyes filled up with joy as they all sat up to their armpits, drinking the river's cool waters. The sun's replenishing furnace shone over them brighter now.

PLAYGOER

Mags bends over Pots who wear floribundas and cut-outs filing into forms: The under counter cats purr with great effusing whiskers; eyes green, yellow, - belisha beacons.

She says "They are needing homes!"

As she points, I sense, see more of them! Ernst counts one hundred, fluffing out like a great moving stack of robes and swishing as multi-coloured ermine, silken swishing!

Suddenly the teeth of dog Pots is a gnashing clam, white with blotches: like ink blows! Blots.. Cats collide - the nails hook screeching over the walls as the white paint screams with spittings, and energetic swinging. Wide their wings - lurch -snap - wack!

Mags is all ogling eyes, oodling over her cats. Smiling unperturbed, she is this gentle hand maiden.

"HUSH!" Her fingers go to his mouth. strokes Pots and holds three, snatching-up fifteen cats together:

How does she do this? All the excruciating beasts collide, collude..draw breath …..

Ernst senses it is she in him, her intrinsic animal -feminine guile and they are coyed, even hushed…cowed toyed, as in a play - familiar as Mags goes everyday in the street, runs after cats or No!

"It is" Mags points: "This one!"

The cat slips. It goes escaping like a snake, slides under her dress…Slips through the door. And Pots follows - leaves the shop to go and run to catch this one!

Mags shouts! "He needs me! I'll be back! First I catch the little scamp!"

Chuckling, she adds jesting, "I'll have to find him or kill it!"

It is gallows humour!

Always so large and so Young! Mags looked at Pots. Both know inside-out the same stuff, yet each comparably more…

"Histories, why bother!" Mags shrugs. Ernst bought lots, so no one minded when he stumbles or keels over.

"Hazards!" Ernst is almost blind but shrewd- eyeing for details.

The far end of the shop contains Mags' wardrobe- an emporium of costume fancies and mostly luxurious outfits. Ernst got lost, stumbling into Mags' outroom.

"Whaz-This???? All theeeze hangings…?!"

His probing fingers vertically sliding down, run through slinky chemise…

"Where, what the..Are you into drying pelts, salmon or snakes skins?!"

Ernst blurts with perturbation, "This sweet smell.. perfume..hiding something?"

Mags stepped in…"I am getting lots of stocks, widening the market!"

"Queer stuff…you have a lot of odd customers!" says Ernst.

Mags took charge.."You can choose, but I want you at the next meeting..my friends are like treating pets well. Believe in having a ball..!"

"That is why Pots wears the frills!" Ernst jokes.

This works, lifts the mood to better cheer.

"And I just hire all these costumes - Robin Hood, Cinderellas and Halloween for pennies, its small beer!"

Erst had collided and set most down across the floor.

"Sorry, I must get those put away!" Mags apologises. Her shop is stuffed to the gunnells. "You take pot luck!" she defers.

Ernst runs a boutique museum and hostelry for pets. It is a start-up holiday home for business owners' pets. The RSPCA granted him a license for rare animals let loose, needing quarantine. From distant parts Ernst gets orders, built good 'cos Mags is a third world trader, importing dried foods - specialising in frozen locust, european wasp. Particular delicacies include squished cane toad, hyena mash and natural endemics - Asian Knotweed, bamboo tips and British Kelp.

"The restuarants can't get enough!"

"What for?" Ernst asks.

"The restaurants use knotweed and bamboo tips as stir fry. Kelp gets used for dyes, iodine and protein. Builders, fabricators, even garment manufacturers also use bamboo for making cloth, bricks. People eat, enjoy the stuff..As for animals..it's a superb food, fillip and blimey..excuse my language..so bloomin' cheap! I import bamboo from China by the ton and it gets a very quick turnaround for fuel and clothing, especially in the North! We're getting bamboo with other fast growing plantations like Hemp here in P M Corbin's post Brexit backyard."

Mags throws up her hands, remembering how Pots got a taste for Knotweed in gravy and afterwards chewed through boxes of orange sauced Ruddy shelduck!

"Were they dried too?" asks Ernst. "I started out with boxes of Coypu, American mink and rabbit and so I got a lot stuffed by my friend Rita..She's a fantastic taxidermist...The orders for good specimens to sell at first far outrun my supply."

"I put you in touch with this specialist ChatTing living in Taiwan who makes imitation animals. His remarkable taxidermy is so alive! Again, the cost...so dirt cheap!" answers Mags.

"We got a world market doing dead stuff, didn't we! The Americans...Donald Trump got a giant sized faux Coypu on his front office desk now I'm reliably told! He says 'My God, Churchill walked next to this creature!'" Ernst laughs.

"They copied his yellow buck teeth and shiny pate! We also fooled...let me tell you - the car boot collectors..I make a lot of money selling artificial imports to these fools, fighting and rocketing each other's prices. We started with little scruple, selling dead road kill to Koreans and Chinese. Avid for these, yet when we siphoned imitation cats and dogs to them...made from Soya, they prefer vegetables to meat!"

"I trade in natural plants - organic is best," Ernest nods.

Mags pats Pots. "This dog, he is my teacher and origami master! My Japanese devotees, all fierce Noh theater exponents, explore scenes in papier mache. They owe much to Pots...!"

"How so?" Ernst looks abjectly dubious.

"Three years ago we had a holiday in Cuba and visited a tobacco farm. Pots loves rolling in snow ; his ardor always in summer turns to rolls in fresh hay. I found where? Pots..I call to despair..he at last I find... where?! Rolling tobacco leaves! Cigars... my Cuban cousins tell me, now are finer, better rolled..preferred pressed, after Pots' rolls."

Ernst demurs, "Perhaps Pots knows more than he lets on!"

"In Japan Noh actors listened to Pots. I mean ...." Mags pauses, "As you know for the Shinto Buddhist life and death commingles...as the masks they wear, bring new secrets and hidden realities open to the wakener, as the actor like the audience partakes and thus perceives..That Pots has this talent to press old traffic victims..."

Ernst quietly interrupts with a muffled cough. "Road kill; those Sika deer and other road runners, yes!?"

Mags had not moved her sight from Pots. "The dog..."

Isha was the leader of the troupe..he turns to me as in a trance.." Eee..AHH EEE! Sooo..Pots has such presence and weight..he has calling to a cold place like a morgue..it is a cold marble slab...We keep respect, honour North gods..guardians of the dead, as living..presences.."

Mags adds "You remember Ernst in this episode?"

"I do, of course.." Ernst smiles relishing the time away."We had sent some samples of artificial made animals..they admired..indeed requested particularly us to send and visit with our own pets.. I wanted us to go and Pots joined us."

"Surrounded by actors, mingling with oriental seers and devotee mache scribes, Pots was watched by all so intently! I had demonstrated how we handle, must respect victims of any creature..it had become a feature of origami..pressed formation..respecting the inner repose of beauty in form.."

"Yes, remind me.." Ernst continues. "As I recall Pots..as he is now..he shakes one ear..it is a tiny tic..is it perhaps..these shop 'small talk conversations,,expectancy getting to him..it brings him down sometimes.. But he is really so proud..while shaking his head. How he jumps up suddenly and goes onto with one straight instant leap onto the marble. He lies upon the road kill, a real Sika deer we had tried to save, found dying on an autobahn outside of north Tokyo..So still, not breathing! All these actors and priests are in enrapture, in awe.."

Mags says "Yes, it is just this..What is happening? Pots at last..like a messenger arrives back..responds wagging his tail and then nips and just with a micro morsel, lumps down over the body. 'Such weight!'"

Ernst adds,"Pots is a miracle worker. And by morning we get the right shape..and get for our deserving Japanese friends gratitude and decorum. 'The animal' they smile, 'it's so peaceful, appealing to them now very happy. They all shake hands, bowing. They say 'Regaining healing, we accept such a life, 'please do send us these. You export vacuum packs. After home, send them straight away!'"

That is why, when Mags, with so much time on her hands does papier mache doll work, uses a 3D printer and with her garnier sachets, rapidly turns out eel worms, bamboo tips, cats..! Pots also is a past master, with so much experience and past history. As a Great Dane he is always made welcome attending Mags' fancy dress parties, recalling 'double outtakes' at The Hundred and One Dalmatians film, down at Shepperton Studios.

Megs' maudlin eyes film over, reminiscing about her part in the HunchBack of NotreDame and more recently, as The Count of Monte Cristo's Countess. Yet for Pots as the most faithful dog to his master The King of Denmark, he merges in plays, the part he knows so well.

Mags says of Hamlet to Pots, "It is not just merely any play to you?"

She fondly pats Pots. "Pots", she laughs, "are you winking at me?"

Pots plays soliloquy; Hamlet is calling him by his silent whistle! He must go!

As he throws his body forwards, Pot's nose scents up and hears Hamlet's voice! This makes him bellow like a wolf, he howls.

"Alas! I miss you so!"

Hamlet calls out a refrain, "Alas Pots, once I knew you so well. Closest friend to me, my Dane. Come back home."

DARKENING SEA

Out of blue horizons voices come. Here, now. Yet in Tobago, it is always like yesterday. In the golden glow of summer's long sunlight. Our ancestors presided upon the ribboning tides. Officiating, yet becalming. A telegram has come. It reads 'Dina is dying', STOP. 'Our children will be homeless', STOP. 'Debts mount up', STOP. 'Come soon Dinka! Save us please'. STOP.

I am Dinka, living in Tobago. I have no money. And I have no passport. My predicament is, I have to help, I have a small herd of goats and sheep. Toni, my uncle, owns the house. I haven't seen him for years. I go to see a man who my friend Sotu recommends. Mr Strami works for customs and excise. He is a straight man I am told, who knows things.

My feet are quite blistered after walking fifteen miles into Tobago's capital, Port of Spain. As I journey, I think of Dina, my sister. I last saw her twelve years ago, when she came over to see the family. She too was born in Tobago. She's only been back once after going to England to marry and work.

I'd never been abroad, having always worked. Tending the herd. I live simply and want for little. My brothers Toma and Dicken taunt me. They have westerner's minds. Toma works for a car dealer on the other side of town. He's married and has three lovely children. His wife Sian is a typist. They go away often on expensive cruises, the choicest restaurants they eat and always dress well.

Dicken is in insurance for hotels and tourism. Although not married, he has a string of girlfriends. And is always out at evening beach parties. Neither brother wants to know about Dina. Toma says 'she made her life there'. He forgets how Dina's late husband once paid off his debts to get him started in business. Dicken is even more curt on the phone. 'Serves the bitch right. After Tobago, England was a total mistake'.

I arrived in central Port of Spain at four. I'm half an hour late to meet Mr Strami in his office. After taking the lift, his secretary asks me to 'sit' while she calls him. He ushers me straight into his room. He greets me warmly with 'of course I know you Dinka'. This surprises me. The man is shorter than I yet looks older. He is clean shaven -unlike myself- and wearing a suit. His hair is gleaming, swept back.

Speech is quick. "We used to dive together with Dina, off Weimann point for pearl-oysters. Your father took us shark hunting. Our families ate Basque many times, barbecuing together New Years Eve."

His warm unhurried voice caressed my memories. He offers a black cheroot and a full glass of white rum. I nodded. My mind roamed in my silence. It wasn't just the ensnaring sea where we breathed, played together and hid away. I remembered all of us children living long days, dipping beneath the waters. Moving at one with the fish.

Toni's father was a fisherman like my own. When they weren't out, they played and swam with us in this paradise of fishes, octopus and seahorses. It was old Sharda my grandfather who told us of the wrecks and golden caves and other islands. There is not a break in our tradition. And it was Toma or Mr Strami leading me to them, to this horizon of echoes… Where all the ancestors live in harmony together.

Mr Strami's voice again urged me to listen: "Dinka, please wake up. I have a business proposition. I must get on now! I want to help. Yet what I have may not be of use…I have many partners. A network you'd call it. I can get you to Dina. For this I take your property. It is, say, a mortgage or guarantee. My partners will lease your house for two months, or for however long as you want abroad. The herd I'll see is cared for, marketed as you wish."

He continued, "For my cut, you give me fifty per cent of the price. If this is acceptable, I'll get you away tomorrow. You'll have five hundred pounds to help you on your way. This is a family agreement only. I can't get you a passport. I'll get you into a container. Yes, as an undeclared immigrant to Britain. You'll be put in the hold of a ship. You'll have to get out yourself after a week. Take your own water and provisions. Your life is in your hands."

Mr Strarmi added, "I'm not to blame, and you can't turn around if anything goes wrong you must understand. When you disembark at Dover, my friend Domo will take you to your sister's address…If you accept this, sign this form. When you come back, your property returns back to you."

Dinka shook Mr Strami's hand. He looked me in the eye and smiled. "We have a deal! Agreed? Tomorrow I'll get a pick-up at eleven pm from your house. Be ready and good luck. Goodbye'. He handed out a bank roll. That's the money, five hundred pounds. In Twenty-five twenty-pound notes."

I left the building elated, pleased with this twist in my destiny. More pleased for Dina though, who now could be helped. I resolved to take the risk. If I got to England, I could work, doing anything. Helping with their mortgage and feeding little Tina, boy Marcus and her two-year-old adorable Sheba.

I rushed home, with little time left. I told no one I was leaving. But I wrote three letters. Two are identical for my brothers. To Sotu my friend, I tell her every detail of my plans. Of what has been agreed. Then I packed carefully for the journey.

I made-up separate packs of dried meat. These daily portions are sufficient for a long voyage. I think, perhaps I'll be delayed, or maybe I'll have to return. Besides these items, I have goat's cheeses, grapes, milk powder and figs. I decided to take only one separate change of clothes. Everything fits snugly into my backpack. My free hands carry the two ten litre water containers.

I leave these things on my kitchen table. Then I lock up the door. I walked to my goat herd that evening. The whole of that last night and the following day I walk them home. Mr Strami had said 'gather them together. Enclose them into your home field. I say goodbye to each one. All recognise their own names with different bleatings. I lie down to sleep at seven.

At eleven pm there is a loud crashing noise at the door. I go to answer and am met with a tall swarthy white man. "I'm Jego, your driver. What the fuck is all this?" He motions to the food, water, the house and herd.

Jego says "this is Dee." Another white man, wearing dark glasses stands behind him. "He comes in to live here. He'll take care of the sheep. The other wagon is empty…"

I interrupted, saying "Mr Strami, he promised to look after them for me."

Jego emitted a raw, obscene belly laugh. "What the fuck do you know Professor! Hurry along and get in the truck or you'll fucking miss the boat…"

But for the gleaming points of the stars, the night was dark. Almost blacked out, the truck's lights were faint. The metal doors clanged, and I swung aboard, dropping down into a fathomless void. Jego said "Here, wear this."

The balaclava had tiny ill-placed slits for my eyes. As I felt around, the roaring truck's engine drowned out any other voices or sounds. Thick diesel fumes rolled backwards in the gloom.

A large crowd of men gradually appeared sitting, packed in together. On the twenty-mile journey only one spoke. "!l don't know if I can manage. I must smoke Ganja and you can't aboard ship."

I said, "Why are you going? Do you have relatives in the UK?"

He laughed. "Are you kidding! I killed a man. I owed a million dollars. He was knocking off my wife. This is payback time. I'd hang or go to the chair for this. I've no fucking choice but take the risk!"

I noticed he had no food. Only one bottle. I said, "You'll starve won't you?"

He replied readily, "You've got plenty, I'll have some of yours! Anyway, when I'm hungry, if somebody's got food I haven't, I'd sooner kill him than starve. Dog eat dog." He grinned menacingly. "Besides, I'm told there's plenty of rats to eat."

Jego shouted from the cab, "Fuck up everyone back there! There must be no more talking. Not now or in the container. Try not to move much either. You'll get all the moving from the sea surging. And crap only at one end! If one of you gets ill, get some water into him to keep alive. If one or more dies, it will soon kill the rest. In one hour, you get inside the container. Get as far packed down the end as you can. There are sixty-five of you. I don't know what the authorities are shipping with you. It's probably pre-packed foods, not live animals or frozen. That is placed last."

He added, "The container ship docked this evening. It leaves at 01.00 hours. The crossing takes 3-5 days, depending on the weather or how busy the lanes are. You'll hear the sirens go tonight and also when you dock in Dover. When you are craned off, they'll open your container. Slip out when the goods are taken. Don't move now until the door opens. Then follow me. I'll take you immediately to your container."

The port was very busy. Lifting gear shifted and crashed about. Haulier cranes buzzed, whining around us. As the tension of waiting grew, the truck's insides blackened. For myself, the prospect of being holed up for a lengthy period-a whole day- let alone one to two weeks, also deeply shocked others. I heard grinding teeth. Cursings and arguments turned to tears. "Hell!" one man spat out repeatedly, "We'll never survive." Also, "We're doomed!"

The tail flap lifted, bathing the interior with search beams. Jego hoarsely whispered, "Go, everyone out!" Then, "On the double, keep low. Follow me!" We heard baying guard dogs and nearby, the shouts of workers. Intermixed ozone and diesel grease smells choked the air. Clustered closely together, we kept moving between the containers. Pincered between black shadowy walls we stayed hidden.

"This is it!" Jego snarled. He pointed to a large iron-red hull with a cavernous mouth. "Get in" he hastened. 'Move right to the back! In twenty minutes these others will be full. When they're gone, it's your turn'.

Like sheep we ran into the dark box. Then Jego was gone. No sooner in, three men fainted. Sickness hit two more. The walls and floors were all oily, damp with a filmy residue. My clothes were running with sweat. "Christ!," I found myself thinking,"'I wouldn't treat a dog or man like this!"

I heard, then watched a man peeing over the three flaked out. Another man cursed, "why you little cowardly shit. I'll teach you to be sick on the floor!"And I heard scuffling of feet. Fists and curses followed. This quickly levelled off. "Shut the fuck up!" came the consensus. The fear of noise was uppermost

Like being out in a battlefield cannonade, some processes are unendurable. Resolutely one by one, the units were filling up and lifted away. The last was peeled off. Our blood changed to icy stone. Then our turn came.

The first lift-truck drove forwards, its lights raking the floor. The truck was as wide as the opening. Its stack of cargo towered up to the ceiling. "Will it ever stop? "I wondered. "Surely it will crush us!?"

Each man pressed back into the rear. Joined into a wall of bone. Had I known, space had to be made, for up to a metre and a half, either side. To allow for ballast shift, the inevitable passage of cargoes moving on the seas.

No sooner had the goods been dumped, all the men crowded forwards. They shifted weight, dropping inhibitions, letting go of pressures. On close inspection, the cargo looked like bulked tins. In less than fifteen minutes stacking had finished. The end of the container was sealed. There was clearly no space for us all to stand together at the back. "Jego is a bastard," men shouted. Having hardly enough room to lie either, men had to clamber over each other or idly stand for days on end.

"Like Jonah I am" reflected Dinka. "From Sheol, the whale's belly I cry. Into the abyss I am cast into the heart of the darkening sea. The flood surrounds me. All waves, billows, wash over me, cast from sight."

The cranes stirred and clutched at the container's sides. Inside lurching men shook. Like a train's cabin, the container bounced upon the track. The freight's sudden shifts of position were alarming. Dinka was violently slammed and jolted up against the cargo of tins. He heard screams as more unfortunate men were first pinned, then flattened.

Again, the crane shuddered forwards, jolted. Returning hesitantly back, it searched sideways for an exact, final position. Haltingly it swung. Then lowering heavily, the last few metres, the container dropped. Inside, boxes jumped, swerving against the sides. Fatally sandwiching ten other men. Only the leaving cranes sawing sounds of chains disguised men's agonising screams.

Holding his bruised ribs, Dinka winced. Pain and fear stifled him. His upper lip was caked in blood and his sore nose felt broken. Smelling sickly air, he drank a mouthful of water and two pieces of meat.

Then the container ship's siren stung the air. The ship's turbines thundered through the decks. Under power, the ship slipped out from its mooring. Dinka sensed the movements increase, surging upward, in overriding pulses. It filled the acrid darkness to over brimming with tirading jarring noise. "I'm hungry," said a familiar voice. Dinka recognised the murderer's voice he'd spoken to earlier. "Is there anyone can help me?" Before Dinka replied, the man said "I'm cradling someone next to me. His face is covered in blood. No, he's not breathing. I shall slit his throat. He'll not suffer any more." The man laughed.

Dinka's heart froze. Never had he heard such a cold gurgling chuckle. "Perhaps the injured man is alive!" thought Dinka. That sound he knew, it was him choking upon his own blood!

The murderer spoke up. "Yes, it's done. It won't be the last in my situation. I have plentiful fresh meat! Enough to last me three more days. Later it will get very cold. So, I'll best start while the flesh is warm."

Dinka turned tentatively to his right and moved away. He stumbled over the first one, then upwards of seven stiff corpses. All had been crushed by that first hugely unbalancing blow. As he walked further around, he found someone alive. This other man was as pleased as he was to meet him. "My name is Toto."

Dinka clasped Toto's hand tightly, hectically shaking it. Dinka gave him water. "I'm Dinka. Isn't this a torment? I'm pleased to meet you!"

Toto tried to hold back his tears, but the sobs shook him. His hurt voice uttered broken from his throat. "There's no one else. been searching…l counted sixty-three bodies…all crushed by the slewing cargoes… Christ!!…what next? l can't stand it…ghastly… this black hole…filth.."

Dinka said "We must rest. If we keep together and take turns at watch, perhaps we can be saved from further disasters. There is a great danger present. On our left is a man murdering and living upon the flesh of his victims. When the flesh he eats turns bad, he'll come hunting us. We must be ready to defend ourselves."

They agreed to stand alternatively for four hours as the other slept. Soon Toto snored. Dinka stood fatigued, restlessly squatting, revolving off the balls of his feet. Lifting again or standing and turning from his haunches, he felt the depths of the ocean surging. Plunging down the fore and aft decks, swelling in vast momentum. He felt the ship drawing and countering the draughts weight; its fulcrum hung paused. It swayed before rolling again, swinging broadly into the vast depths.

Dinka heard the growling engines, pitted and whining through the folding currents. The hull turning and rolling, swerving, and balancing in slow lumbering passage. The vast crashing waves sent up foaming flying spume.

"It is awash all over the boaT" he thought. As his drenched body took the reeling motion, swaying as the floor keeled, he grew used to the trickling seepage washing across his feet.

All sense of time disappeared. Since sailing, ten hours have passed. He thought, "l hoped with daybreak this container might let in some light."

Thinking it was time to alert Toto for the watch, Dinka reached down to waken him. His hand touched a figure. Instantly he recoiled. Toto was cold and stiff. Dinka's had caressed an open wound. Standing up, Dinka felt complete revulsion engulfing him, choking him in this blackness.

"This serpent's darkness" he rued giddily, a chamber of horrors... Then Dinka felt a faint movement behind him, the pulsing sense of another man's flesh. He felt heat. Then this other power lunged, flailing to overwhelm Dinka. He smelt the attackers gasping exertion. Of stale, rank breath and spilt blood. A monster's frightening evil presence drew nearer.

"Who are you...?" Dinka cried out. As he did, he bounded over Toto's body and ran off towards his right. However, as he leapt, he felt a hand grab his left ankle and fell. He thudded heavily onto the floor. Dinka had the presence of mind to use both feet, recoiling back. Lunging heavily, Dinka felt the impact. His boots kicked into the assailant's face. Jarring leather dug into flesh.

The man wailed out, "Fucking bastard, you've smashed my face!"

Instantly his hands let go of their hold, quelling the spewing wound. Dinka regained his footing. But he felt the floor lifting. The whole hull was rearing upwards. Beneath the climbing ship, huge cresting waves clawed, building suddenly. Hastily Dinka crouched down, clasping limpet-like to the wall. Attempting to magnetise his hold.

Rearing up to the fore, the ship continued rising. "She's going!" he thought. While his feet dangled, Dinka's hands tightened. Sure enough, as the floor angle fell away, so the moving cargo slipped, inching down. Under such momentum the tonnage dropped,

screeching back to the far side. The weight was immense. It had to subside again before recoiling.

The screeching noise of planing-steel couldn't disguise the howling voice, disappearing. "Oh save me... Jesus sake...I'm falling...!"

The tossing ship had entered its severest test. The storm raged on for two days and nights. Dinka fought to stay alive with every fibre of his body. Yet even he succumbed, becoming soon unconscious in the struggle. Quiet, alone.

It was in the quietness of nightfall when the container was opened. The light blazing in, awoke Dinka. He blinked. A huge suited blond figure stood at the entrance. He carried a long black baton in his hands.

The man barked. "You're bloody Dinka aren't you, I know you. I have your description fixed in my head, yes the goatherd! Why aren't you dead? I see the rest of my boys are. You'll wish you were when I've finished with you! You'll pay for their deaths. Get up. You've got some work to do. Don't you know I'm your new owner? Dina's been dead for ten years. I've got ownership of her children. I am Domo. You work for me. You're my slave."

IDO

The world where Ido lives is full of fantasy, a long forgotten island off the coast of Japan where man rarely sets his foot. Hokishwi is the name of this small universe where Ido and his friends go through incredible adventures...adventures that need to be told...and there it goes...

A tiny tadpole sized boy, only 7 years old, Ido is always curious, from dusk 'till dawn, he lurks around, investigates and not alone, but with his friends. Somehow he knows there's more to this world, and he takes every challenge with tiny steps...'cause he's so tiny too.

One shiny morning, he comes out of his Holt, and ventures out onto the warm sands of the beach. This is his favorite spot...the light and warmth caress his skin and he gets to play with all the other animals who make their way out of the salty waters. This time, he spots this huge 'herd' of greenback turtles, so busy and don't observe his presence, so Ido runs towards them.

"Hey there...how do you like this lovely morning?" he asks the turtles who almost all turn their slow heads towards him.

"It's fine?" Ido bursts into laughter feeling playful and energetic.

"We're busy!" An old turtle replied and they all left minding their business.

"Yeah...that was fun" Ido mumbled to himself and went towards the edge of the water; he knew there would be more activity, and since he was an energetic, so full of life, the tiny tadpole sized boy, gazed at the dolphins that were chasing each other through the waves...

"That must be intense..." Ido thinks and waves at the Dolphins who actually see him on the shore.

"Yooo...come in, the water is great!" one of them shouts. Ido smiles, and even if he knows that he could never swim as fast as dolphins, the thought of playing with them cheers him up and so ventures into the sea. The water next to the shore is full of seaweed...Ido's favorite food, thus he takes a few bites and chews calmly...

"Hmm...this tastes great...I don't understand why others don't like it!" he thinks as he tries to swim into the open waters.

Truth be spoken, Ido was not so great at swimming in deep waters. His friend Aki, the crab who was still chilling on the sand, saw what Ido was trying to do now, and kept shouting at him.

"Ido…watch out, the currents are acting crazy this morning!"

Ido heard Aki and looked back winking… "I got everything under control"

The problem was that Ido only thought that he had everything under control, and in reality, his life was really in danger. A fishing tackle popped up out of nowhere catching Ido…all his friends and all the other animals sweep away! Ido is trapped, with little chance to escape, therefore he starts to scream for help… those nets are tight and tangled.

"Heelpp…someone please help me…anyone, pleaseeee heeellpp!"

The creatures living in the sea are terrified by any kind of fishing tackle and swim away as fast as possible, yet this time a squad of brave fish came to help him. They pull him out of the net and carry him on their fins close to the beach.

"Now you should be safe!" they all say at once and Ido cannot find his words to thank them for their deed.

Ido feels reborn now and swears an oath to himself that from that moment on he's gonna help anyone who is in need of help. He's gonna give back to the 'community' exactly the same way those brave fish had done for him.

He looks at the waves thinking of the horizon, imagining stuff and wondering how things might be beyond that. Ido is at peace now, but his heart is restless like the waves and he hears the voices of countless animals ringing in his ears…

"Ido, please come and save us, we're being poisoned by all these plastics…we're dying here, please help us breathe again!"

It's clear as daylight to Ido now! He has to do something about…and this might be the greatest adventure of his life…it might be dangerous, lots of unknowns but still, he needs to do something and help the other creatures.

"Be brave, and careful…" Ido's mother tells him "I know you can do this…I have always known deep down!"

Ido smiles and embraces his mother… "I'm a bit scared," he mumbles.

His mother smiles "It's normal, but you needn't worry…it will fade away…this fear!"

With this in mind, Ido jumps on a plastic bottle and is pushed away from the shore by the currents. His mother is still on the beach waving at him; Ido smiles, waving back, then turns his attention towards the vast ocean in front of him.

"So much water…" He mumbles and sees this throwaway styla foam and speeding microbeads. Ido jumps on it as this appears to be a lot more stable than a plastic bottle.

Now he can finally sit relaxed while drifting on the ocean currents. It is unclear to him where he is heading, but this is not really a problem to him…the more disturbing thing is the picture that was unfolding in front of his eyes no matter where he looked.

Debris everywhere, plastics and other materials were choking the ocean waters causing all sorts of problems for the creatures living in the water. The fish and everyone else was trying to cope with this 'new problem', but for how long?

Soon enough, Ido realizes that he is not alone and countless other creatures are traveling alongside him. He is amazed to see the multitude of species, in far greater numbers than he had ever seen before.

"Where are you going, stranger?" A huge bluefish asks him. The fish was swimming with his friends forming a well-coordinated team.

Ido shrugs; he does not know where the ocean current is going to take him eventually.

"I am curious to see myself!" Ido replies with a big smile on his face.

"My name is Kanee," the big bluefish added, "Don't tell me you're going to meet King Neptune?!"

Ido's eyes widened suddenly… "There is a king out there?" he wonders but does not get to say another word; the big bluefish starts smiling.

"You have a long way to go…I wish you the best of luck, my friend!"

Ido thanks him politely and watches how the fishes swim away; he touches the water with his hand… the water feels warm, and salty and seems to be filled with minuscule creatures that abuzz with life in all directions.

He tries to look under the sea, because he is convinced there's more than meets the eyes, yet Ido's eyes are too sensitive and cannot cope with the salt. He pulls his head back up immediately and touches the water again with the hand. The water vibrates…strangely…it looks like something indeed is happening down there…but what is that?

Ido wonders and ponders on his floating foam and prays that there's nothing too dangerous. "Where am I going?" he wonders, confused. "How big this ocean can really be…what if it does not have an end and I will float like this forever?"

What Ido did not know is that his questions will shortly get an answer…because from deep down, right from the bottom of the ocean, the coolest creature was right about to get to the surface.

The ocean trembled, and the water looked like it was changing colour…and then there were those awesome voices.

"We welcome you to our grounds, come join us, friend, as we'll go diving…swimming up and down, we recycle the ocean, bringing new life into this changing climate!"

Ido looked down and only feet under his floating foam, he sees great numbers of blue whales swimming in circles around him. He's shocked and amazed at the same time…

"Wow…you are so big" Ido mutters "The biggest thing I have ever seen in my life!"

"We know, and we have a responsibility compared to our size! We are the guardians of the ocean, we are protectors of the ecosystem!" The whales spoke all at once and then one after another, they started emerging to the surface so they could breathe, needing air in order to survive…

Ido quickly understood that whales look like fish but they aren't really fish…there was something special about them.

"Who gave you this mission?" Ido asked curiously.

The whales happily reply…

"We have had this mission from day one…nature itself gave us this mission and it's been eons since we started doing it, and we keep doing it even if now it becomes harder and harder with all this pollution.

Ido began to understand the greater picture, he started meditating, thinking about what needed to be done…but then the plankton itself started talking in even greater numbers…

"We are important too…you know?" the ocean itself spoke, "We help clear the plastics and all those bad gremlin carbon poisons; without us, everything else would die!"

Now it was clear to Ido that every creature in the ocean had its purpose. Big or small, everyone had a job to do so that the ecosystem worked perfectly.

One of the blue whales that had a very interesting mark on his fin flew up in the sky then slammed the water on the side.

"The ocean is a beautiful thing!" Said the blue whale "And we need to keep it like that…alive and safe! Our Namas Pois Plume, so rich in iron and nutrients, is fertilizing the plankton; by bringing food to the upper zone where the light penetrates, we help the plankton thrive, multiply…and in return they feed and remove tons of carbon dioxide from the ocean."

The things Ido was hearing were indeed incredible, and he felt even more, the urge to do something himself.

"I wish I could contribute too!" Ido said to the great whale.

"Your time will come, don't worry…you'll get your chance to change the world!" the whale replied and helped Ido shake off his unease.

"I hope you're right…" he said and saw some oysters and clams jumping from the water and onto his floating foam.

"Who're they?"

"They're friends too…and offer great help in cleaning the oceans!"

"We're Cockle and Mussel," the oysters said smiling and got closer to Ido "And we have a great plan…"

Everyone was all eyes and ears, Including Ido who was curious to hear what those brave oysters had to say.

The whales and other fish in the ocean were listening carefully to those two oysters… an amazing picture no doubt! This showed that oceans have no hierarchy and everyone there matters; their lives are all important and they all suffer because of the massive pollution created by mankind.

"We're gonna build huge barriers, the whales, the fish, the oysters, clams, the corrals, octopus and everyone else." Mussel spoke "We need to stand united against this phenomenon and fight for our own survival because if we stay idle and watch it happen, one day we might not have any room to swim or food to eat! Our collective effort should be enough to collect all the debris and plastics that are choking the oceans!"

"And what then?" Ido asked, a bit confused.

"Then, we'll recycle them and never ever allow it to happen again!" Mussel added "And we also need to act now! Every second we delay means another life lost and lots of problems for those who are still swimming! It's our duty to take care of our home…cause, after all, the ocean is our home and we should protect it."

The water of the ocean was vibrating, as all the creatures agreed; starting with whales and ending with oysters, they now had only one mission: to clear the waters of the poisonous pollution.

Ido was happy to see all those animals united into a common cause; he felt a part of it too and this meant he had to bring his contribution. He thought about it for a while, and then this great idea came to his mind…a brilliant idea!

"Listen everyone!" he said with a loud voice. All the animals paid attention to him…from the big blue whales to the small oysters.

"What if we build these semi- circular dams and let the ocean currents do the job?"

Ido continued making everyone curious. They had never heard such a bold idea before.

"Semi- circular?" the oysters wondered…and Ido felt like he should explain better.

"Yes…semi-circular, like round you know…half of a circle and when all the plastics are gathered in one place we can complete the dams into a circle, like little islands. This way all the pollution will be trapped safely and we can remove it from the oceans for good.

"This sounds like a great plan!" the big blue whales exclaimed "We should do this!"

Now everyone is happy because they had a viable solution; and started building those floating dams as fast as one could say Ido!

Cockle and Mussel cheered for Ido "You're so smart Ido, we're lucky to have you in our team!"

Ido smiled, shook his head and got to work immediately… and the best part about it was that they were going to use pollution to clean pollution.

They grabbed big pieces of plastic and other kinds of debris, tied them together in that semi circular shape and placed the dams in strategic positions where the currents were stronger.

As soon as all the floating dams were finished, results started appearing…and they were all excited!

"I can't believe it…it's really happened!" Mussel said happily.

The blue whales on the other hand, wanted to give a hand and make the cleaning process happen even quicker. They started jumping into the air and then splashing the water creating giant waves that would push the plastics towards the dams even faster.

With every passing moment, the waters looked cleaner and cleaner…just like they used to look before people started polluting them.

Ido looked through the clean water and he could see all marine vegetation and animals that were swimming along.

"We thank you Ido, you are our hero!" They cheerfully fill Ido's heart with pride and happiness.

This had indeed been a job well done, but it was not over yet as Ido and his new friends had to complete the circles and secure the plastics before they could dispose of them.

They split into teams and started building the other halves of their artificial made dams. Soon, the ocean was filled with small circular islands made up completely of plastics and other debris.

"What now?" the other animals asked Ido.

He knew that they could not let those plastic islands float onto the ocean for eternity…they needed a permanent solution! And Ido, again, came with a brilliant idea.

"What if we take them away?" he said. The animals were a bit confused.

"Take them where?" one of the whales asked Ido.

He smiled and tried to find the best words to explain to them: "The islands are floating, right?"

The animals nodded as this was fairly obvious.

"What if you push the plastics to the shore…and there we can take care of them for good?" Ido asked his team and they thought of this to be a great idea.

"That's right… let's do it!" the whales replied "Come on Ido, hop on…we're going to have a fast ride!"

Ido laughed and jumped on the back of one of those blue whales… Roger was the name of the whale and he was So Big… I mean, Ido looked like a little pebble on Roger's back…but size did not really matter in this effort after all, everyone's contribution was equally important.

"Hold on tight!" Roger knuckled and started swimming and pushing one of those plastic islands.

They reached the shores of Hokishwi in no time. The inhabitants of the island were terrified at first when seeing those large entities getting closer to their beaches. They all started running scared looking for places to hide, but at a second look, they saw Ido riding a huge blue whale.

Their fear turned into curiosity now and as a result, they all came closer to the waves to see what was going on.

Ido jumped off Roger's back and into the water… dozens of whales were lined up next to the shore, each pushing a plastic island.

"What is this Ido?" someone in the crowd asked.

Ido smiled, "We finally decided to clean the waters of the oceans; this way all animals can live a life of peace and harmony."

Their eyes widened with amazement…as everyone thought cleaning man made pollution nearly impossible.

Ido's mom was there too, looking proudly at her son who was now a hero of the island! She was crying with happiness and everyone else was cheering his name…

"Ido… Ido… Ido!" The crowd shouted with excitement while carrying Ido in their arms.

He deserved it…no doubt! His curiosity and courage made it all happen, and even if he was not the biggest or greatest creature on the island, Ido proved that one can really change the world if he had the guts and determination to do it.

The oceans could breathe again now, and all the animals could smile…and all due to a tiny tadpole boy who really believed the world could be clean and natural again. A dream comes true, with great efforts and unity.

HELTER SKELTER

Touch down, grounded, safe-landing. Navigator terms, like terra-firma. When you are up, you are up! When you are down-you are down!

Mat walked on air. Blood free, sky walking on the wing. Doug his dad flew. The old by-plane is a Tiger Moth. Red and very old. She waved her arms. Waggling in friendliness. But she could drop suddenly. The air prop suddenly cut out! That is why they wore parachutes. And hoped for goodness for safety and getting the old gal or bus home.

Double Vision-Treble Trouble. Doug is a natural flier. Both father and son love Patches, their mongrel dog, with his motley black patches and big splotch on his tail. When Mat brought him home-a rescue dog, flying seemed crazy. After all, he only had been doing the wing walks because The Circus would die without someone prepared to act.

Circuses turn somersaults. Mat and Patches got into training. Doug's pilot's eyes scored the closing in crowds. Swerving, arrow-like plunging out of the clouds. Audible as the shrieking winds were the escaping gasps as the plane spun near to them, upwards reaching to the stars.

Patch bounded up and down in the trainer's elastic harness. At three to fifteen meters drops, Patch proved he could get stable on all four legs. With Patch ready, the harness was lifted to a circuit movement. He was able to move aloft. The dog rose and turned swinging about, then swung steadily and elevated to his powered flying wings!

Mat took to duck and hawk twitching to gain aeronautical insights. Doug and Mat took turns jumping, holding the dog and then pitched him in his solo chute! Mat had overcome his own fear of heights. Doug led him and Patch for some more jump and wing walks training, so they went together into a nearby old empty Tower block.

The escalator was broken so they routed up the stairs. The wind whistled down the stairwell. On every flight of stairs, the shaft seemed trickier. Suddenly Patch smelt air and took off. His legs bounded forwards. Hurriedly, Doug and Mat ran after him.

Parachutists and pilots quickly vanish. All visualize flight paths, tumbling corridors and rushing of rotating cumulus..Tethering rip chords, vying altitudes into rising slip stream thermals; Mat felt the cold of icy alto cumulus. Reaching the twentieth floor he glimpsed Patches trailing harness disappearing over the tower wall…

Doug tugged him back up. The heavy lead-like ballast lunged heavier and caught around Mats ankles. Lurching then staggering, he began spinning down. Patches now in complete free-fall saw the blurring pitch of windows passing him train-like, running down and flying vertically skywards.

Just as Patches was shutting his frightened eyes, he heard a bird's call. 'It is I Tiga, fear nothing Patches!' The kestrel Tiga was able to catch, then pull-up Patch's lanyard, drawing upwards, soaring them into another flight path. Patch flapped his ears. As he did, his fur rose and his tail lifted like the small tailgate version of the Tiger Moth.

'Am I flying solo now Tiga?' asked Patch. The hawk had stopped pulling him and replied "Yes, you are in slip-stream, go faster…' He saw both Matt and Doug touching down in their parachutes a long distance behind them. Patches had his feet nearly down. He watched keenly; Patches began ascending his body off from the ground.

Mat untangled himself and ran forwards. Suddenly he felt a tugging and a man shouted 'You are Taboo! Get lost, Go!' Mat swung into a fight. He got the man by his trouser legs in a pincer movement to the ground. 'Who are you?' shouted Mat, hissing angrily.

'Of course you don't know me. Herr Doug does! We fought in the Fokker wars. He wears Red, after he shot down Captain Ball…Nien, The Red Baron is killed. Ah..my introduction. I am Count Zhavrov- You have never met a spy. My aim is only one, to stop your escapades. Ze War endings. To bring your flights of mercurial fancies to an end and quickly kill this Circus bubble!! '

Mat pinned the spy, but the Count pulled harder and slipped out of the window. A white parachute unfurled, drifting away west upon the gusting breeze. Very strong, Mat excitedly dragged himself upwards through the tower. In next to no time, he stood upon the roof. Far away Mat heard then saw Doug riding very high in his Tiger Moth, veering way Northwards.

Below was a Black Cross. Mat blinked, shrugging unsure. He asked out loud, 'Is that a bird?' Then glinting, moving and comet-like it grew in speed and sped upwards towards the old plane.

Something familiar pressed against Mat's legs. Patch sized him wildly up and down. In next to no time, the dog ran around his master and tied him up with the leash! Then Patch took off, running away. Patch ran even faster to gather even more speed. Mat rolled behind him, bumping over the roof!

'What are you doing?' shouted Mat. 'Let me down you crazy dog!! You must let me use my phone! Help!!!' But before Mat could fight or do anything Patch had reached 'Super-Dog speed- his tail turned like a propeller and his ears flapped faster than a coxswain's metronome beating out Oxford's oarsmen to time.

Patch had one BIG purpose: instinctually he had to get up. The old biplane, like a small endangered ladybird, clung to his vision. Out there his senses drew the dog's muzzle- smelling engine oil. The rumbling aeronautics from the sounds of splintering wood made Mat also listen. More surprising, Mat saw Patch rise! He was taking off, taking to the skies and the lead of the dog held him as he swayed, going upwards. He was rising as though on a swing, carried into the air below Patch skywards!

Doug circled the aerodrome. The air chute changed direction, flagging him to land due south-west. Fraternisation between all sectors of air arm corps was a court-marshalling offence. Cross lines to meet the enemy for duals on the ground was unheard of. The Circus that day Doug voted to entertain was beyond the ken of any Kaiser Officer, let alone shared by open declaration from double-spies. Yet Doug had purpose, wanted blood, dug in his spurs. Old flames of camaraderie, horse play or devil-may-care had been cast aside. The Circus must perform!

The build-up of throwing down gauntlets, declaration to dual and rendezvous before dawn was a ruse. It became far more sophisticated than that. The spy that Mat had met was the son of the Red Baron himself. His twin brother Ruiz got maimed picking up the ticking bomb, timed to go off as he unwrapped the challenge to meet in the old drop zone established by The Red Cross.

Sickening bubbles of venom, coronets of fatigue held. The chassis of both planes creaked as they both lifted skywards. Was it an auspicious challenge? The sky was warm, yet unpredictable. Both planes circled; the black plane carried Count Zhavrov with his poisoned lance to admonish and pierce Doug's balloon. Meanwhile, Doug fatefully sped forwards obliviously cresting the heavens. He smelt only the start of rain and enjoyed the ruddy storm clouds scattering the first autumn rains.

Some things inevitably happen. Silk and paper rose in heated profusions. Kites seized in a tremor of moon light burning at highest episodes turned twisting ever higher. Patch had his eyes widely focused by the light from the moon and other attentions he spoke of. He was surprised by a moon frog!

'This frog', Patch said 'Smiled like the Moon, always shines back at me. It said 'You are a flying yogi Patch. Go and save your Master Doug.' A query arose in Patch..he had not asked the Moon. 'Why had she called him the Moon Dog?'

As a dog he differentiated between metal and fluid..silver bubbles..but his own powers thrust him powerfully forwards into a ballistic arc coursing upwards. The lighting rains of myriad bubbles like bands of green and red lifting fronds shot upwards, riding the ocean winds.

Countless bells were floating past him in musical orchestrating interludes. Everything was tingling alive and blinding.

A flare of lightning hit the metal black smoking cross. In a flash of fierce force, a red light shaped as a red claw lifted. Patch saw a red coloured giant crab..he was sure that was what he saw. The great crab slowly lifted his timely deft craw and struck out at the black plane. As a scimitar it fell and flung the black cross down. The plane briefly staggered then dropped swiftly out of the sky.

The crash and the fizz of so many breathing bubbles like a great wall of soda slammed furiously up and then down, crashing into a wave of fermenting embattled mud. Count Zhavrov sat down, his mouth was fizzing red in a trail of bubbles escaping. 'I am of the age of field stations , mobile encampments, pontoons… Mien Zooks! So much, all too much, this smoke and battle fatigue..'

The Fokker he was still galvanized, showed power. Like the old war horse he was descended from, he was earmarked with guarded fighting zeal. Cloaks, flapping canvas, bivouacs fell before the wash-out rains flooding across the rain soaked lines. Wave upon men fell; bedded in, then lay drowned out by the deepening tide of floods…

Doug leapt out of his plane and Mat shared the parachute. But it was Patch's timely mastery, his action who got to them. The parachute was shredding, silk filaments like a man o' war jellyfish left the meshing chute breaking, mushrooming apart. As he dropped down under the figures, his fur lifted movement held out, carrying him and Mat slowly down. Cushioned above the dog, they had hung before they had eased into the waves.

A crown of spume, the white canopy of the parachute sank blanketing the coral bed, hiding the place where the Count had sunk. Doug had been prepared and even scoffed. 'I knew, yes the old account had never been settled until now…he was after contrition and I had wanted one more flight before the circus we were ready for. Now we must go to the coral island.'

He pointed. 'It is just beyond this reef… Nowhere is like this place, of oxygenated waters, a peace haven of bubbles! We must celebrate and camp! We all are beyond hatchets or misgivings here…!'

WHAT IS EATING YOU

The fir trees outside my Woodbridge Base are all frosted today. I stare at them. Mother says, looking over my shoulder: 'Breakfast is ready!'

But Josey says 'I don't feel hungry. I only want some of THEM!' 'What!? Mother says. 'You can't eat?' 'You must...'

She slaps Josey's hands reaching to open the window. 'You can't eat frost, even if it looks like ice cream... It's so really not! Come and sit down. Here's your bowl. You really must eat..If you'll just sit down, you can have ice cream - a spoonful with yours!'

Joseys got that taste again. She's also been having awkward feelings lately. Saying strangest things: blurting 'All's super and sloopy, slum-dunky darling -far out!'

If anyone she knows answers back, she reposts with 'What's normal? Or shrugging, 'It's just: 'incontrovertible.. Super, darling!' She puts up her fists, swearing when she's told she's angry.

Josey knows they're talking about her, both friends and family. She doesn't care as she is so like her cat 'Dinks.' Far-out, curled up laughing..smiling even when she starts to get a little bit uneasy inside herself. She's even then blissfully so aching with laughing. When alone she curls up and can't stand up! That is so normal for her. She wonders, wouldn't it be nice to be Abnormal doing and being like everybody else, for a while, just even a minute!?'

'Stickies, Why have them. First it was her eyes. Mom says 'I get these. You'll live!! What is it about mothers and sharing? She also insists 'Josey we've both 'photogenic brains!'

'What are you on Mother? `` She had raised the game with our 'hypersensitivity to smells, tastes. And don't even begin worrying she insists. `` We 've spongy brains, absorbing everything. That my daughter is unique! I do feel for you, Big time! '

Josey nods, just to shut mother up, get her to go away. She's unsure, 'cept she knows she has these very weird 'Thingies' going on..Combinations, she calls them. Josey just now can't quite work things out. She's heard some calling it 'Synesthesia..' To her, she's fixated on her brain, mixing everything up. Scents waft and sneak-in all around her brain, getting her to choose the most horrible things. She's doing routinely what others would never do.

Josey no longer cares. She's this new entity, working overtime…Switchbacks, hooking my addiction..Must have..To do…Loving to try everything..Right now she's sticking with Vanilla. The smell and taste makes her senses wholly run riot. Signals falling in so that's the taste ..I. must have all the time!

Daphne's her friend. She's very funny and so together, cool! She is also into 'Her Thing!' She loves and can't do without everyday die-for-itsy-pink and' syrupy dreamy -drives -me-mad donuts!' 'Hmmmn the smell; I must buy them all the time..

Daphne 'Far -out, an' Fabulous! 'They're aching-good," she says.

She's losing weight. Josey recalls last week Daphne's ice popsicles. Like sunshine shoots regularly after falling rain, she follows fashions and switches to her next craziest fads l

Daphne 'Why do you stick with Vanilla..It's so old fashioned Josey?

'I disagree, it's not for m e any longer the look or the buying..Rather I go for the smell..' She adds..'Why do you use that scent?'

Daphne looks hurt. 'Donuts.. smell..They're fun!'

Josey: 'I taste, I actually exude the donut smell! Vanilla! It's me, isn't it..I seem totally built of these ingredients!!'

'The other day you had a taste for eating dry bread. 'Daphne quips: 'Then you tore up that book.' Other stuff is more important..' That was your comment..So weird, it's wicked! You were doing your homework.! I remember now! We were laughing..so much my sides were bursting. When we stopped, I was hungry and I said we must go get some ices.

'You go! '

'I said, 'No Josey, we both must!' I forced you to get going for a walk. We ran when we nearly got caught lifting stuff in that store! '

Cos you said 'Josey replies, 'If I don't come I actually…know what you are like, you'll do something. So Weird! What is wrong, I don't get it Daphne!?

'How can you do what you get to do I have seen you roll up some pages of paper.. You blankly stare back at me Josey. And you say 'This is what I eat..It's good enough, really tasty! I can't stop it..It tastes good..Gotta eat Vanilla!! You start to bite..'Stop I say!! You even bite me. 'I must eat!' You're eating your homework!

Mother ate coal. That was your reply! She told me! When she was pregnant! That was what she needed, it was her thing!'

We got only ten yards and you started clutching your stomach..'What's wrong Josey, are you hurting?'

'I feel it, it's kicking me..So deep it hurts..it's alive! Kicking me inside!'

'You're sixteen and pregnant!'

'It's his..!!! Hal's..He started me..We shared everything close…..I didn't know at first..I thought yes I really like him..And he's so addicted to his taste for Candy   A cheap thrill! he said. 'Vanilla ices Yuuukk!! 'I grew close 'cos he loved what I did. I never wanted to hurt or say no to him. I got so into him, eating together the same dreamy Vanilla stuff!.'

Daphne: Laughs. 'Hal is the ring leader selling skunk. He's still selling; he's safe now in jail.!

.He got you hooked on Vanilla…?'

Josey 'Yes, with Vanilla he fed me skunk I got close to Hal, I leant to love the taste for that also…'

Daphne: 'Dont tell my ma if I don't tell yours, okay??? I sure love that stuff!.Your tiny baby!

She laughs. He's living on Skunk as well!?! '

CLAYMORES RATTLE

"Fiddle-Sticks! Kith-Kin be jiggered!"

Old wobbly knees ClayMore kept stray animals. He fed them up and opened his holding for old and young to enjoy. They have handler's for donkey rides, camel capers, and ostrich runs. ClayMore drew in crowds and had many old fogey's come to visit with his appeal of, "Take up the offer, our animals need your support! Just as your own health improves, going out with them for your daily ride, we fix it for yourselves!"

Many asked or wondered, "Prosthesis, Be Gone?!" Some heard of fleecing; others fatefully harbouring the feeblest expectations, kept away. Those joining, gathered in the tableaux dotting the land.

Aunty Brisket, proponent of rocking or muscle-tremble therapies, made the steps and platforms gently tempering. At first, the most ailing of the gentle folks sat for the view in the Swiss Mountain gondolas. They lifted in a swaying motion, meant to be elevating and a tonic to their 'nervous systems.' Gaining low gravitational thrust, fresh air, improving their spatial awareness, they set the old sallow skins a 'tingling!'

Dio, Fio and Fum are brown bears with characters of unusual proprietary and tenderness. Dio always bows and smiles. Then on meeting, he claps his hands and walks with a waddling, gentle way. The three are Russian Steppe bears, who so often broke out of captivity. They got set free, doing several acts for ClayMore. 'Skydiving', and 'Rocking The Ages', they sing along a memory of themselves together, striding freely and enjoying wild times in the woods.

They had introduced ClayMore to the Crocodile Walk Fandango. Cakes for tea were set out for supper times, along the walkways. A gentle nip here, a rewarding bite there: Grandpa and Gilly had another taste: they were so taken, they wanted lots more. The crocodiles provided seats and tables- you rode on them, swerving round this way and then that! As you rolled, you felt your body swaying but safely harnessed in firmly. The curving backs of the crocodiles, slowly inundated, while pouring the teapots. As they rotated, freshly arriving cups and tea cakes came serving the spell bound passengers.

The crocodile affably announced: "Look at these 'Thinking Man's Chimp's!'"

"Roll Up, come see Sirrah! Hey Mr, Mrs, He, She!"

The old Orang-outang named Dag was nodding and smiling, then talking. Dag stood at the entrance of the ride. Titled: 'Anything Goes-What Can-Does Happen.'

"Of course it's important. We shake hands. Look in the mirror. See, Is You!"

Images in these mirrors shone; Dag did something unexpected. ClayMore tells visitors, "He stands next to you, Dag is your friend. He invites you in to look in his Hall Of Mirrors. Look! A wonderful change overcomes. The old 'You' returns. Strangers laugh again! Taller, becoming supple!"

Looking with brown big eyes intently widening, Dag held the window of the glass as it stretched, opening the mirror further. Milly and Grandpa stepped through to a different place, somehow drawing them in. The skin and faces changed while stretching bodies. Both entered renewing time; their wrinkles turning to smiles, emboldening them.

Out in ClayMore's garden two by two, Dem-Bones and Clip-Clop the grey elephants pranked. Cartwheeling, they turned pink from army field grey, surprising visitors. Eight African elephants did slides, the strong trunks lifting several lucky goers in the baskets. Others applauded the fun-runs which included doing 'rollie-pollies' as 'we oldies' get wrapped-up in carpets and twist over, undoing the rolls!

ClayMore announced, "I'm proof this works! - No more sciatica, lumbago or dreaded arthritis. Roll your bones flexing and new bodies do emerge!" Sticks and callipers flung high as they joined in, rumbling and tumbling down hills.

Three-legged races running so slowly drew cripples in droves from their wheelchairs. Locked in with out-and-out paralysis, they even managed somehow a few steps tied together; others found confidence to run, going far further than they could remember. The stray dogs ClayMore befriended, came bounding about, jolting and imbuing everyone with much laughter and mad barking amusements.

"Life is", says ClayMore "A neuron market." The flea circus vied with the spinner tops: somersaulting gymnasts took to be in charge. The air crackled with electricity, as the energy charged up from the ground lanterns. Surprises were everywhere: children led the wizened up ramps. They leapt across spaces, twisting down and swung above the stationary. Hanging and flying with élan upon the swings, jumping hand to foot and tumbling down into the jump nets, helping to land or bring up again and link into further flights!

ClayMore kept his pride and joy: the garden of playful devices, for those who felt their needs weren't properly met. "This is my ice glacial garden to melt frozen hearts." Sure enough there were slides and tensile ropes, with assorted sizes of crampons for ascending steep rock faces. Tucked away in a private rose garden, prayers were offered and letters left, for hoped-for invitations and answers.

As at Lourdes, the place was tidy but never over organised. Callipers, prosthesis, walking aids no longer required, lay idle and bore witness. "Bury in our garden a wish, be rid of waste-limbs" ClayMore advocated.

Bees and honey; people came with desires and flowers, planting themselves in ClayMore's garden. Rarely speaking, a few of his reflections got passed around. "Final is false. Alive living consolation! Lifeless, Nut-Trees bud. Healing delivers. Old today is born tomorrow..!"

Top-notch, by root and branch -with bending ears to bowing knees, upright stretches found new-found confidences. ClayMore fought tide and time vigorously. He brought in wrestling, with new changes into bearing and position here. Ramps went up, with bars to bend up to. And springs, both steel-coiling and as drink-shoots sited and adorned the place. The new found hope sprouted artificial beings. Gatherings of wax-wings and woodpeckers cut out vertical marks like trophies for those who had turned back their pain and decrepitude, finding new joy to their lives.

On the ball, ClayMore's Grandpa Whistler was really old. He climbed up and down daily to live in the tallest tree-house. It is, he insists, the "best and only way to stay young!"

Feeding only on berries, pollen and nuts, the squirrels helped feed him during snow-fall. Not yet hung up his 'spurs', this ancient leprechaun popped-up for a glass of cheer, roistering with his most-young 'old pals.' Whistler taught kick-about jujitsu, aikido, boxing and kendo. He'd found a sprightly old fox to box with, or fought with one-hand the three bears.

ClayMore pulled levers. A whole season the animal park closed. Sometimes he got bemused- never reckoning any equation of confusion. He'd hear the stream bubbling through his park, coursing and singing like children's laughing voices. Every day growing louder, the water's bubbling all day long and on through the night.

ClayMore rolled it up. "Only those who try it can explain what is done inside."

He said. "Sharing and sheltering; throwing between them this ball… Going back and forwards, brings fire, life is searched for. Pass anointing to each other over and over again…"

The tails of the curling bright and glossy squirrels run, yet always returning. "This" says ClayMore, "Falling with dreaming desire, is how age is! It lies for a season buried as a nut. Then in an instant, Spring grows and builds again."

He continued laughing, "See now the nuts lie buried, snow is on the ground. But there is more , yes here is knocking - you and I share this sound! Like a clocking, clicking dull-wood resounding noise of the woodpeckers hollowing-out, pecking the trunks…Yet it's something else!!? Squirrels are playing bowls. The pegs are the shells of people, buried here now, that they too have left their hollows. Buried up to their heads. The squirrels rejoice to be so near to the shapes of humans, normally so hard to stand!"

ONE OF US

The Public conveniences beyond the west facing pier at Folkestone are rundown but clean and welcoming.. Labette Bilt the Proprietor is the French hostess, par-excellence! A most diligent attendant. All the surfaces of the tiled partitions are sparkling white. On all sides, rivulets of rose scented cologne mixed with eye-watering bleach follow her as she mops and stringently sponges up and down the floors, over every surface..

In and out, visitors come through, some more hurriedly or else stride nonchalantly in, staring inwardly bemusing. Such a glance has Labette, She appears unaware. She sees, yet heeds only to her care. She carefully keeps time and carries on so exacting..As the interior quietens Labette rests in a hammock, up in one corner. Here she appoints herself a resting place.

"What-Cha!!" So convivial..

Or 'Hello dearie..Nice Day, lovely Sunshine..! Obsequious nods to the little maid for the free seaside service. Busy always for them and awfully tidy.

Other Men march in and bow, saying 'Bless You!'…

Dropping by more frequently, old boy Tommy wears his Argentine war wound making him increasingly scowl,.while half held coughs make him spit involuntarily..

Labette reminds: 'Use Hanky Dearie..!' But he can't help..

She adds: 'Prostrate, is it? Thought so!' She counts his faltering feet.. He is eighteen steps in and out.. Shuffles, is gone..

Labette is tireless to serve. Beneath her starched tunic, her body moves with unequalled study.

Her eyes, small..black..dancing..watch all movements with acute exactness and dominion..All the men..The intros and outros are her customers..She has the intensity of an insect's devotion: Domestication..Domestos: are Labettes singular attendant cares.

Labette's instincts forbid to step over the threshold. Many run errands past this cubicle of glassy surfaces. Blind keepers offer dogs, volunteering to get sundry toilet supplies.

In strict spidery patterns, Labette busies back and forwards, crossing all floors. No one sees her scuttling over walls..then lastly crossing over the ceiling. Her inner thorax. repetitiously covers every dimension of these enclaved..glassy spaces.

Using corn-starch, brought in by visiting host flies, she has a ready ally in the blue electric box, crackling then discharging every last flight. How else can she manage..Fears come to her like a tide rising, bringing screams inside. Warm air pervades the toilet space. From summertime fields humming insects pour in..

Kegan, is such an efficient electrician, "Where's it going Miss?'

She points.

Where else?

Kegan looks down at her diminutive size and asks - to himself:

"Is she shrinking? Best not speak loud as she's getting frail.' She never speaks. Maybe Labette is deaf..or just a bit Do-lallay.!?

He speaks again. "Busy are we?' He smiles..Feeling unusually..curious..He ascends his ladder and quickly drills and completes the assembly..

She strives tirelessly to remove any offending mark, mite or offending murk as daylight climbs strengthening. Light casts shadows; her evening real 'watching-hour '.begins. Deeper changes occur in Labette: Now she can steady herself; her yellow rubber gloves rest. For a brief moment, Labette is idle.

She scuttles about when the latrines become empty. Her legs stretch, elongating: as a telescope, craning for new speckles of dirt…

Like all other arachnids..she's a shepherd; the kind of European order that uses stilts to better observe wanderers or flocks from a distance…

'She reflects: 'More ancient am I than men..'

Never hesitant to wipe away any other spider, she swiftly. gives no quarter: Both son and her father she bound in threads. Left high and dry as bundles like cotton balls they hang high up there in the apex of this room. Lifting is easy..Few notice either the arching webbing branches, where she closes down..nightly resting..

Now it is dark, the toilet sinks begin gurgling. Toads emerge..Labette stays still as they start, shuffling slowly forwards one by one..

The air quakes. Across the floor they slide slowly moving towards the side door open for vagrants coming and going for shelter.

Labette watches as the trickling mud trails across the white tiles..One by one the frogs and toads flow out the door.

'We all have much in common. Frogs, toads and men.. A dying species.!'

Labette sighs.

'Women freeze eggs..and bank sperm..Personally I welcome these new generations of froggy toads, new men!'

ANOTHER FESTIVE SEASON

Old St. Nicholas dusted off his red coat, chuckling with glee at the remnants of tinsel still hanging about his collar and the white-sugar mice tails dangling out of his pockets.

"How times have changed" he thought; "presents aren't what they were, much lighter and so many more."

Despite the increasing cold, the dark was lit by the aurora-borealis, the "Northern Lights ", shimmering as incandescent rainbows upon a white lake of endless snow, as starry as silver ermine.

Egor the Finn and his Serbian half-brothers, Petervich and Karl looked after the giant deer herds, walking with them over the tundra wastes on their migrations. For the last three weeks, the animals had trekked down from the north lands, to feed on the abundant pastures of winter mosses and growing lichens.

Petrovich always drank more vodka at this time of the year.

"For the coming festivities brothers."

The three friends had a small cabin, one of many besides the Tanya river.

Egor did his part, logging and feeding the stove, while Peter cooked and Karl served or sang and answered the door. They had just sat down for their meal after a long day, when there came a loud knocking upon their door.

"Come right in white hare and silver fox, what brings you here?" inquired Karl. His nose was especially red from drinking and his eyes were watering from the fire and from peeling onions. The fox called Frenzy spoke up shrilly, for he had a toothache again from the recent blizzard. He held a piece of red scarf wrapping his face.

"That twittering eagle-owl says he's stuck on the old Yule log and he's not budging!"

Brear the hare looked cross but said nothing.

Petervich cut in, "The Little runner knows that is not it! What are you saying Frenzy? Come in both of you and taste our early mince pies, before we hide them in a secret place outside before Xmas!"

Brear came up to the hearth and how quickly his eyes shone, and his frozen whiskers lifted, as the bluish-snow on them melted.

Frenzy soon sang, nibbling upon his hot pie, dancing to and fro from each foot, swinging with excitement around the glittering tree in the rooms' corner:

"Now elfin fairies gather mistletoe, carrying baskets as they go, Heaped-up with red holly berries, Apples, pears and ripe cherries."

Gulping for air, he continued:

"To the tallest pine trees,
The Elfin' spells they wreathed,
Lighting candles brightly with frost.
Sparkling the decorations, ivy tressed.!"

Something suddenly made the fox stop singing, and his steadied face looked up intently, with his right ear lopsided towards the frosted window. t

Tap, tap', now the tiny noise was just audible to everyone. Petervich stumbled forwards in his usual lumbering way and unlatched the door a little. It took all his strength to stop the gusting gale from sending him flying backwards.

Fortunately, he was joined in his curiosity by Karl and Egor, pinning him at either shoulder. Quickly Frenzy and Brear were attached too, at his feet! They were all used to listening.

A snuffling, shuffling gigging sound came closer. Then, before anyone spotted anything, a deep voice and then more laughter addressed them. "May we come in and join the party? Jeepers-creepers, boy do we all need some cheer!

And what's this I hear about confusion? Tut, tut, Santa going on strike; not enough larch wood for the sleigh, so the pine-martens and beavers are saying! And what of the rumours? Of Randolph with toothache, his fear of heights and needing a rest, always hoofing it! Seems a funny thing, what with Claus commemorating the anniversary of his sainthood soon!?

These voices came from five cold animals. They were all met with, "Come in Chip the chipmunk and Tinder Tapir, and you too Brock the badger."

Bounding behind them came Nutty the squirrel, also Pinko pig, an excellent candle-maker.

"My how you all have worked, getting all those presents ready for the children" laughed Egor; his tears of pleasure were running fast onto his beard.

He went on, "Claus himself was only saying to me the other day, I've heard glad news that cheers me, the English have started to light their fires; I can' t stand cold feet! "Al so, "More people than ever are buying Xmas trees this year, as if I don' t have enough in my load already. I have to make room, you know! Last year I had a sky train of fifty sleighs waiting beyond the Black Forest; this year I have tripled the number."

Peter added, "Of course in his distant travels he uses the stars, picks up the fruit and nuts buried by the squirrels and holds special sessions with flying cranes, using also the gossip overheard at kindergartens and primary schools, by mothers waiting to collect their children.

Just then, as he had poured out each one a small cup of steaming hot fruity punch and passed it all around, a gust of wind blew up and shot open the door. They all looked up and everyone gasped with the same exclamation, "Look, it's Santa Claus!" For silhouetted against the cold sky, was the unmistakable fast-train of Father Christmas, riding out overhead with all his deer and sleigh! "For sure" said Peter, "the festivities have begun early this year!"

Milton Keynes UK
Ingram Content Group UK Ltd.
UKHW052220110124
435898UK00007B/190